To my dad, who had his guiding hand on my shoulder and will remain with me forever.

Yalda Afshoon

# THE TIDES OF THE PAST

Two strangers who were entangled in the stories of their past and future were drawn together

AUSTIN MACAULEY PUBLISHERS™
LONDON • CAMBRIDGE • NEW YORK • SHARJAH

**Copyright © Yalda Afshoon 2023**

The right of Yalda Afshoon to be identified as author of this work has been asserted by the author in accordance with Federal Law No. (7) of UAE, Year 2002, Concerning Copyrights and Neighboring Rights.

All rights reserved. No part of this publication may be reproduced, stored in a retrieval system, or transmitted in any form or by any means, electronic, mechanical, photocopying, recording, or otherwise, without the prior permission of the publishers.

Any person who commits any unauthorized act in relation to this publication may be liable to legal prosecution and civil claims for damages.

This is a work of fiction. Names, characters, businesses, places, events, locales, and incidents are either the products of the author's imagination or used in a fictitious manner. Any resemblance to actual persons, living or dead, or actual events is purely coincidental.

The age group that matches the content of the books has been classified according to the age classification system issued by the Ministry of Culture and Youth.

ISBN – 9789948802556 – (Paperback)
ISBN – 9789948802563 – (E-Book)

Application Number: MC-10-01-9266665
Age Classification: E

Printer Name: iPrint Global Ltd
Printer Address: Witchford, England

First Published 2023
AUSTIN MACAULEY PUBLISHERS FZE
Sharjah Publishing City
P.O Box [519201]
Sharjah, UAE
www.austinmacauley.ae
+971 655 95 202

# Table of Contents

| | |
|---|---:|
| Introduction | 7 |
| Chapter 1: Meetings and Greetings | 9 |
| Chapter 2: Career to Follow | 22 |
| Chapter 3: Growing Up | 34 |
| Chapter 4: Incomplete Introduction | 41 |
| Chapter 5: Woken or Asleep | 46 |
| Chapter 6: Solitary Party Hall | 52 |
| Chapter 7: Grab the Opportunity | 61 |
| Chapter 8: The Time After | 72 |
| Chapter 9: Fallen Behind | 79 |
| Chapter 10: Confusion Is Nothing New | 91 |
| Chapter 11: Sharpest Words | 99 |
| Chapter 12: Darkness Grows | 109 |
| Chapter 13: Secrets Stollen | 123 |
| Chapter 14: The Unforgettable | 137 |
| Chapter 15: At A Loose Ends | 147 |

Chapter 16: The Alternate Route 159

Chapter 17: Final Is Not the End 166

Chapter 18: From the Author to the Readers 180

# Introduction

It was four years ago, and the ground was frozen and covered in snow. Mum instructed me to go outside and begin clearing the walkway with a shovel; it took me 5 hours to finish arrived fatigued and, regrettably, could not feel my fingers due to the cold! Dad contacted me after I went into bed after a hot shower and said:

"You have a call from a gentleman who wishes to speak with you." It was too late for any guy to call me at that hour of the night, but when I took up the phone, he identified himself as Sir Malik, a well-known artist recognized for his gorgeous artwork and amazing words.

I didn't grasp it at first while he was introducing himself, but as my eyes widened, I realized who he was.

I couldn't figure out why he had contacted me as he was so calm and nice during our talk.

He mentioned a lady who was my high school English teacher and who had sent him my first novel (She Had It All).

After finishing the novel, he expressed his want to know who the young writer with the magical touch was. He has now chosen me to write their narrative, his and his wife's story.

At the time, I was pretty surprised, and my voice was trembling. I explained to him that I am new to the field, with no experience, and that I am too young to be chosen to write about him!

He just said, "Yalda, I'm offering you a rope to pull yourself up; if you don't take it, someone else will."

He was right, chances like this doesn't happen easily and I was too lucky to have one.

The only issue was the distance; I lived in the south of the country, while he lived in the north.

I promised him that I would attempt to visit him, but traveling such a vast distance for a girl my age was difficult.

I accepted the task, but I was concerned about whether I would be able to give the exact quality that Sir Malik requires.

I praised him for the wonderful opportunity, took his phone number, and promised to be there as early as possible. I couldn't immediately articulate how I felt.

I believe I yelled for 60 seconds to get the adrenaline out of my system, then did a crazy dance with my blanket.

After I had finally relaxed, I began arranging the entire journey with my father.

My mother was first furious and kept asking why I should be the one to go through the inconvenience of traveling, but my father eventually calmed her down with his magic words!

Greetings, dear readers! I added my own spin to the story, but I genuinely attempted to convey the realism of the situation.

I hope you enjoy it as much as I did.

Yalda

# Chapter 1
# Meetings and Greetings

*The travel time had finally arrived after days of planning. My father chose to fly instead of taking the bus, which took roughly 17 hours. Father couldn't bear leaving me alone and wanted to be around me at all times. Actually, he was more interested in the story than I was!*

*We agreed to go to the hotel once our plane landed, rest for an hour, and then get ready to travel to Sire Malik's residence.*

*It was not difficult to locate his house once we arrived at the block where he lived. Except for Sir's house, all the houses in the region were like royal houses and as fancy as they were in movies.*

*Sir's house was quite basic and old, yet it was nonetheless lovely and, I assume, held many memories.*

*We arrived in front of the gate, but I had no idea what I was doing there. I received a strange feeling out of nowhere, I was afraid, and I requested my father to return to the hotel. Immediately, the gate opened, and Sir Malik emerged.*

*He was tall and gorgeous, and the perfume he wore took my breath away. He shook hands with my father and asked us in, though my father apologized and said he needed to go see some old friends and would pick me up later that evening.*

*The building had a pool in the center and was surrounded by evergreen and very tall trees, as well as several roses of all colors.*

I was invited inside by him. I entered the living room, which was brimming with Sir paintings, the genuine ones, not the ones I'd seen in shops, on book pages, or on postcards; they were too lovely to pass up.

His wife entered after a time. She, too, was tall, with blue eyes, red hair, and fair complexion.

I felt I remembered seeing her somewhere, but I couldn't place her! "My name is Natural, but you can call me NAT, please take a seat," she added as she welcomed me. "Malik informed me that a young writer will be visiting our location to write about our ancient and modern."

I sat next to her on the sofa and told her it was my pleasure to be of help to them, and I appreciated them both for believing in me and giving me such a wonderful chance.

"Believe me, no one could do it better than you, or you would not be here," Sir Malik replied as he stood up. He then dismissed himself to go finish off some work.

"I am so thrilled there is a lady who is going to write about us, it makes me feel more secure," Natural stated as she sat near me.

"It's best if I start from the beginning," she added. "My real name is Gloria, my mother is from Spain, and my father was born and reared in Paris. They first met at a party, fell in love, and married six months later. I was an only child who had been lavishly indulged."

When I was about eight years old, my parents decided to take me on a cruise for the holidays. I was terrified of going on the cruise at the time and refused to join them.

They didn't have any other choice than to enlist the help of their newlywed friends to look after me for the next seven days till they returned.

Tragically, I realized on the third day that their cruise ship had toppled in the water, killing all of the passengers. I didn't understand what it meant at first, but I gradually realized they were dead and would never return to pick me up!

I was yelling and shouting if anyone was around for a few months, wanting to drown myself in the bathtub or lock myself in the room for days!

My host family intended to adopt me until one of my blood relatives turned up, at which point I would become their daughter.

Regretfully, I was absolutely out of control; I recall filling the bathtub with water and tossing a few toys in it, thinking they were drowning and I was attempting to save them.

I was blaming myself because of their death, was thinking if I would have insisted more, they wouldn't ever go on that trip or If I were with them, I could have somehow saved them.

My new parents found it very tough to look after me. They tried their hardest to help me get recovered, but I was becoming worse every day.

My Aunt (father's sister) finally showed up one day and invited me to accompany her to the north. stated she couldn't come pick me up earlier because she was too preoccupied with the funeral.

I honestly didn't care where I was going or who I was staying with. She was one of the country's most powerful businesswomen, with properties in every state.

Shaadi was her name, and she was a widow who was much older than my father. I recall her coming to our house for a brief visit and then leaving, presumably because she needed some documents signed by my father.

She gave me one of the biggest rooms in her palace, since I didn't want to go to school, she arranged the whole school at her place to prepare and educate me.

Still, I was reeling from the loss of my parents and had no desire to entertain anyone or engage in discussion with her.

I requested Shaadi to stop calling me Gloria; I was giving myself a boy's name every day and trying harder to dress up like them.

At supper with my aunt and her friend one night, she mentioned to her friend that my attractiveness is natural. When I first heard the word, I insisted on being called Natural.

One of my greatest ambitions was to grow up to be a boy. I imagined that if I had been a boy, I would have been stronger and could have swum quicker to save my parents before they drowned.

Shaadi let me do whatever I wanted, and she never said no to me.

At the age of fifteen, I had a boxing coach; this was the age when all the girls started dreaming about their futures, falling in love, dressing up, applying cosmetics, and so on, but it was completely opposite for me.

I've decided to become a pilot and have asked Shaadi for assistance.

She was first stunned and shocked, but she pledged to do everything she could to assist me in achieving my goals. When I turned 18, she sent me to the city's capital to begin my training.

It was unusual for a woman to become a pilot in our day, and you would never see a female pilot in the country; I was one of the first three female pilots ever.

Our images appeared in magazines, and our interviews were frequently broadcast on television. They treated us as if we were celebrities.

After 8 months of training, I was given a one-week Christmas break and returned to my aunt's house.

Shaadi had prepared the palace for my arrival and had lavishly embellished it. To be honest, I never liked them, and she never asked my opinion on anything.

On Christmas Day, she informed me that we will be receiving a rare visitor from afar; he is a prince who will soon become a king. I wasn't sure why he wanted to meet me or for what purpose, but I agreed.

Albert was his name, and he had roughly ten servants accompanying him to our venue. He came in for supper and apparently gave me a big hug.

I didn't feel safe in his embrace, and his touches caused me to move further away from him.

My aunt was irritated with me for not dressing up and showing up at the table in a pant and shirt, but I didn't mind because ladies' clothing was too hard for me.

After that night and their speech, I realized he was here to get connected to me; he wanted to show the world that he had the first Pilot woman and therefore increase his popularity.

He attempted to spend a lot of money on me during that week that he even presented me a car for the new year, although I couldn't fathom myself being around him.

I was completely uninterested in him. He had the potential to be a fantastic buddy, but he desired something more, which I couldn't provide.

I was completely uninterested in him. He had the potential to be a fantastic buddy, but he desired something more, which I couldn't provide.

I recall him whispering to Shaadi's as I was leaving home that Natural was a sick girl who needed good treatment to recover.

After a few months, I discovered that he had married a princess whose father was the monarch of a western country.

It made me question if there was something severely wrong with me after that! I attempted to take more classes and operate more flights until I collapsed during one of my training classes and was forced to take a temporary leave.

I returned home knowing that no one had expected me. Shaadi has already left for another nation for business. In her lonely life, I never understood why she needed so much fortune!

I was never interested in learning about her life or the types of businesses she ran; we rarely spoke because she was always busy and I was always incompetent.

I was bored at home and decided to go to the library, which had roughly fifty thousand or more volumes. I wondered why I had never been to that location before.

I began reading a wide variety of books until I came across one that altered my life forever, and it was placed in a separate corner from the rest.

Shaadi assured me he was the best, and she kept mentioning his works as if she knew who he was!

I began to wonder what was going on in the novel the second time I read it, and I realized it was Sir Malik's book.

It completely transformed my mood, and I began to fall in love with him and his works. I believed I connected to him, I slept with his words and awoke with his thoughts.

I began ordering all of his books and reading them over several days.

I wished to visit him one day and tell him how I felt; it was my biggest hope at the time.

I was astonished since I had turned down a Prince's love and the future, I could have with him in favor of chasing a dream I didn't know was true or not!

Sir Malik, tall and chubby at times and thin and dazzling at others, sprang to mind. I couldn't care less whether he was wealthy or religious.

I was enamored with his thoughts and words, and I knew that no regular person could conjure up such a miraculous tale.

She paused in her speech and looked me in the eyes, saying, "It's dreadful to be indecisive, not knowing which group or gender you belong to."

When I was with groups of boys, I reminded them that I am a girl and that they should not make dirty jokes, and when I was with girls, I wanted to show them how much higher they could go.

I just wanted them to know that there is nothing males can do that woman can't.

My entire life has transformed since I first fell in love with Sir Malik and his novels.

Unwanted and beyond of my control changes were taking place inside of me.

I no longer wanted to be a pilot, but if I quit, my aunt would no longer continue supporting me, So I resolved to continue my education while also looking for the love of my life and tracking down his location.

Shaadi invited her pals one of those days and requested me to join them. I entered the hall wearing one of the garments she had bought and placed in the cabinet for me, Shaadi shrieked, scared me, raced towards me, held me, and whispered, "You remind me of your mother, and I'm sure your parents would approve of your attire." She seemed nice to me, but I wasn't used to receiving compliments.

When I heard their name, I felt awful and hurried upstairs to change into my old jeans and blouses.

Shaadi approached me and inquired as to what she had done wrong. I said, "I don't want to be a woman, I don't want to be soft, I want to be tough and bold."

She took my hand in hers and said, "We don't get to choose our gender, but we do get to choose our destiny and improve our habits."

She stated that she is celebrating something extremely important tonight since she has finally found someone for whom she has waited a long time.

She sat on the side of my bed, crying for the first time, and said:

"I'm completely responsible; it was my trip that drowned them. Your father called me a few days before they left, asking if I might book the best accommodation on my European cruise."

"I was delighted to assist him. I was food poisoned and taken to the hospital the night of the incident. I had to wait months to get back on my feet. I was afraid to confront you."

"I tried but failed to keep myself occupied so your thoughts wouldn't annoy me. I heard you weren't doing well and didn't want to abandon you."

"I am responsible for the deaths of hundred twenty people, but I got over it; in this society, you sometimes need a thick skin to exist!"

"It was no one's fault," I kissed her and murmured. "Natural, my darling," she said after wiping away her tears, "you want me to erase everything, yet you can't do it yourself. I've watched you struggle and suffer for all these years."

"Even if you were a lad, you couldn't do much when you were only 8 years old! However, at your age, you can assist me in a variety of ways!" (How could I help her if I had no idea what she meant?)

I felt my heart was no longer heavy after crying so much. "This is your mother's scarf, which I have conserved all these years," she added, pointing to the old boxes in my cupboard.

From that night forward, I said farewell to the masculine world and entered the female one.

I began to dress in a variety of women' attire. I could change my garments to female's outfits, but changing my character was more tough.

I used to talk and move like a man. I recall the first time I tried to balance in long heel shoes and twisted my ankle! I didn't want to continue my studies and was becoming increasingly depressed as a result of not being able to reach Sir Malik.

Shaadi noticed my alterations and inquired as to what was going on. I informed her that I had fallen in love and couldn't stop myself. She couldn't imagine I was the one who said it.

"In love with who?" Shaadi inquired. I had the impression she already knew but wanted me to say it.

I burst out laughing and told her so. "He is a writer, and I have fallen in love with him and his writings despite the fact that I have never met him."

"Oh, so you adore his books," Shaadi responded with a smile.

I informed her in a clear voice that I had fallen in love with Sir Malik the writer, and she didn't take me seriously. I expressed my feelings and informed her that I can feel him in his words, be seeing him in my dreams, and can't picture a future without him!

She inquired one more. "How can you fall in love if you have no idea who he is or what he looks like? What would you do if he was married with five children?"

I told her that I couldn't answer all of her questions until I met him.

Stupid girl, "As you stated, he is a writer, he lives in the world of fiction, this is his work," Shaadi remarked. "None of them will tell the readers at the start of their books whether they are single or married."

I added: "If I discover he is married, I will not worry his family and will return to my mundane existence. I need to find out where he is and learn more about him."

"Please give me some time to think and don't do something dumb without telling me," Shaadi urged. "In the meantime, go back to the camp and finish what you've started." Actually, she readily agreed to assist me, and I was grateful.

The next day, I packed my belongings and returned to my training camp. I had one more year to complete my training and obtain my pilot's license. Everyone in the camp respected us.

The ladies were the first to go for the fresh fly, and I had the highest schedule, so I could finish the course faster than the guys. I liked how the ladies were emphasized there and given the respect they deserved.

I brought roughly twenty, Sir Malik novels with me, so I won't be lonely. While reading those novels, I had the impression he was conversing with me and sharing his memories.

Eight months have gone with no news from Shaadi in the camp. I was losing faith and growing sicker by the day; I couldn't understand she couldn't or wouldn't find him for me despite having all the influence in the country.

I was resting one day after a long travel when I heard I had a guest. I arrived at the site and spotted Jamal, one of Shaadi's buddies and business colleagues. I had seen him many times visiting Shaadi and talking their business; he was Muslim and used to invite us to any celebrations he had in his home.

He inquired about my health. He stated Shaadi had informed him about Sir Malik, and while he didn't want to get engaged at first, once he realized I was real, he couldn't say no.

Sir Malik is one of his best friends, he said, but he is now out of the country on a tour of Europe and Asia to meet and greet his admirers and promote his new book. I believed I was dreaming since I was so delighted that I didn't know what to do but hug him, which made him laugh.

He continued, "He affirmed he will be back in two months after conversing with him yesterday." I inquired if he was single. Fortunately, he stated that he is unmarried. "I knew he'd been waiting for me all this time!" I stated.

Jamal said, laughing, "Sir Malik is a little unique; he isn't like the other males and has a fiery temper. He has changed several house maids because no one can stay at his home for more than a month."

"He is now without a servant and has requested me to assist him in finding one. His last housemaid mysteriously quit for no apparent reason. I thought I could present you as a house maid to him after conversing with Shaadi and learning about your affections for him," he stated.

"You can only get to know him this way. I persuaded Shaadi that this is the only way to realize he is not normal and let go of your affections for him."

I was surprised to see the hall door open and Shaadi enter. I embraced her. She said that they were on a business trip. I asked if her would let me work as a servant in Sir Malik's residence. She responded, "Do you believe your parents would have allowed you to do this if they were still alive? Do you understand what it means to be one of the country's first female pilots? You'll be starting your formal flights all over the world soon, and you won't have time for all of these."

"Shaadi, you know how much this means to me, please permit me to do it. I will go for a short length of time, will be graduated in four months, then will take a break for a few weeks, I believe it is the perfect time for me to visit Sir Malik House." I explained.

"What if he attacks you or attempted to take advantage of you?" Shaadi remarked, who was quiet and appearing concerned for me.

"I will only agree to two scenarios: first, I will only offer you a limited amount of time, which will be three months at most." Even if he is too sweet to deny, you must begin your official flights when this period is completed. If you agree in front of Jamal, I'll also let you work as a servant in Malik's house, but I'll need all the specifics, and Jamal will keep an eye on you," she said.

I was overjoyed and kissed her, after which they both said their goodbyes and went. I couldn't imagine it was really happening; my vision will soon become a reality, and I will be able to live with, eat with, and enjoy my love's companionship.

I couldn't sleep until the morning that night. I was feeling conflicted. My mind was racing with ideas. What if he refuses to hire me as a housemaid, or if I get into a fight with him and flee? What if my aunt was right, and he tried to take advantage of me in some way?

# Chapter 2
# Career to Follow

Natural took a big breath and expressed his need for a little pause. She returned with some sweets that she had earlier baked, which were excellent and still warm, then she continued.

I finally completed my training and became a licensed pilot. I couldn't recall anything about my graduation day; all I wanted to do was collect my belongings and leave.

When I arrived at Shaadi's house, I was surprised to learn that she had planned a surprise party for me and had invited all the wealthy individuals I had never met or seen. She only wanted to brag about her niece, who is now the country's first female pilot.

I pretended to be having a great time. I walked to my favorite area in the garden, sat beside the pool, and was looking at my reflection in the water when I heard Shaadi calling me.

She urged me to come in since it was going to rain, and I noticed her approaching me with a jacket in her hand.

This was the first time she had shown concern for my health; I had spent my entire life playing in the rain and snow, but she had not dared to contact the workers to bring me in; I had no idea what was on her mind!

"I understand how you're feeling," she said. "I was young as well. I was seventeen years old and in love with our neighbor's son, who was ten years older than me."

"When your dad discovered of my hidden relationship with him, he requested that our father locate an ideal match as soon as possible. I begged that they allow us to be together, but your father refused to do so. He was implying that love is like a fever that passes in a night.

"Love will happen after marriage, I was informed! I was compelled to marry the governor's son, who was mentally ill. Our fathers were great friends, and I was a birthday present for him.

"Because of his illness, he died soon, and I became a widow! His fortune was the only thing was left for me." She explained.

"I couldn't forgive my own brother, especially after realizing that he had married for love. He took everything away from me before following his heart. Many years have gone, yet I still remember my love.

"I looked everywhere for him. I had no idea what my family had done to him when he departed! After that, I gave up and resolved to do what I was intended to do, which was to generate income!" She added.

"I reveal all of this to let you know that even if you return heartbroken, the world will continue to turn. Take it all in stride and keep your faith. Before you depart, come to church with me and let's pray for ourselves and the women around us tomorrow." Her words sank into my soul.

I felt awful for Shaadi because, as tough as she appears on the outside, she is just a little girl who wants to be loved and protected on the inside. She was correct. Whatever happens, I should be prepared.

That night, I was wondering about Shaadi's background and the secrets she kept to herself.

Maybe that's why she came to see my father every two years.

I began packing, but I had no idea what to bring. I requested assistance from one of the servants and seek her views. I even received assistance in how to dress and apply make-up.

I got up early and went for my daily five-kilometer run. Before we went to Church, Shaadi requested that I eat something. We were both quiet during breakfast, immersed in our own worlds.

The driver was waiting for me, and Shaadi hugged me and said, "Jamal has already contacted him and informed him that a new house maid is starting today."

I was stressed the entire time, unsure of how or where to begin! What happens if he recognizes me? I just wanted to be regular, and I was hoping things would go smoothly.

I fell asleep in the car on the way from my Aunt's house to Sir Malik's, and when I awoke, I found our car parked in front of his house. Before anyone noticed us, I stepped out of the car and instructed the driver to leave.

His residence was unlike any other that I had ever seen. Two lion sculptures stood in front of the house, which I thought were remarkable. I rang the doorbell and waited; eventually, the gate opened and he exited.

He gave me a serious look and asked, "May I assist you?"

I was still staring at him, unable to speak; I believe I was tongue-tied at the time!

"My lady, can I help you?" he said again. "Do you think you're lost?"

"My name is Natural, and I'm here to help you with the housework," I said, shaking my head.

Sir Malik: "Are you sure you are too attractive and immature for the job?"

I told him not to worry about my appearance; I was here to serve him. He then welcomed me inside by throwing his shoulders up.

It was a large garden with massive trees, each of which was probably hundred years old, and broken sofas were erected in one corner and covered with red colored blankets. They seemed unsettling.

He welcomed me inside the house by opening the hall door and inviting me to settle on the sofa. He then went upstairs, giving me time to look around.

Jamal was correct; the house had gone months without a servant. The sofas were dusty, there were spider webs everywhere, the dining table looked like a library, and the chairs around it resembled a shoe rack! Oh, my gosh, I had no idea how I was going to clean up all of this mess! I was thinking to myself.

I recognized his work when I saw gorgeous paintings on the wall. I looked for the kitchen but couldn't find it. Sir returned, still in his pajamas, appearing precisely the same, only his face had entirely transformed, there was no hint of friendliness, and his hair had been combed!

He sat next to me on the sofa and remarked, "I'm not sure why Jamal selected you for this career? Has he told you anything about me and my perception?"

"Yes, he has clarified everything, sir," I answered with a shake of my head. "After all he described, you were ready to work for me?" he asked, still unsatisfied.

I said that I require this position and would like to gain some experience. Jamal decided that the best and safest location to begin would be your home.

"Are you aware that I am alone in this house?" he continued. "Is that acceptable to you?"

Yes, I said once more.

Then he requested me to accompany him so he could tour me around the house.

There were only two rooms on the bottom level, one of which was full of antiques that he didn't want me to approach since they all belonged to his parents.

The other was a guest room, complete with a bed, chair, and a shattered wooden cabinet! A few carpets were also folded and stored in the corner. Then we proceeded upstairs and found two bedrooms, one of which he claimed was his office and the other his bedroom.

He informed me that I was not permitted to enter any of these rooms and that he would take care of them. We then proceeded to the back garden, which was pretty lovely, with a tiny round pool and a ring of red and white roses all around it. He responded, "These are the only good things in this House," pointing to the flowers.

In the back garden, there was a kitchen. He stated that this location needs a lot of work. It was the first time I'd seen a house with an outdoor kitchen, but I suppose such designs were common in the past. We both came back in, and he was expecting me to say my goodbyes and flee, but instead I asked him when I could start. He asked if I still wanted to work for him after seeing all of this.

He obviously wanted me to alter my mind and leave right away, but he had no idea I had come to stay, not to leave! "Have you worked anywhere else?" he inquired.

I said, "No."

"You can easily make a lot of money as a supermodel or actress. Why do you wish to work as a housemaid for such a low pay?" he asked.

"I told him that the experience is more important to me than the money; I don't care if I'm not paid; I've always wanted to learn housework, and Jamal knew that because of my appearance, I'd have trouble, so he offered your place, as I previously stated." He was still unsatisfied.

When I inquired whether it was acceptable if I took the guest room downstairs, he said, "Are you planning to stay here for the night?"

"Yes, I have a habit of getting up early, so it will be extremely difficult for me to continue travelling from my house to yours; I will be on the road the entire day, if you don't mind, please allow me to stay."

All downstairs, kitchen, and yard are yours as long as you don't bother me, he replied.

Then he went upstairs to get ready, leaving me with all the chores ahead of me and my thoughts on Jamal. He stated that no one can stay with him and that he expects me to leave as well, but I must remain strong, as nothing is impossible in this world.

I stood up in front of him as I saw him coming down the stairs. He explained, "It's preferable to keep the formalities at bay; you don't have to stand up every time I pass. By the way, I'm a Muslim, so I hope that's not a problem for you!"

"Not at all," I responded with a smile, "we're all the same, don't worry about it." After he was clothed, he looked absolutely stunning.

I began in my room, where I had a plethora of undesired items for which I had no idea what to do. After that, I went to the hall and then to the front lawn. I cleaned the leaves from the walkway, washed the stairs, and watered the plants.

I finally made my way to the kitchen. I opened the windows and began removing expired and ruined food from the refrigerator and cabinets. Following that, I cleaned the kitchen and wiped down all of the windows. I also swept the rear garden and watered the rose plants surrounding the tiny pool.

I was hungry, so I checked the time; it was almost evening, and I hadn't had lunch yet. I searched the kitchen for a box of crackers and brewed some tea. I fell asleep on the table while waiting for my tea to cool.

I opened my eyes to see him standing in front of me after hearing him call my name.

"Have I come to the right house; someone should wake me up too!" he exclaimed, surprised.

"I just finished my job!" I said with a smile.

He said he had to do a lot of shopping because I was going to remain there, and then he went, saying he would return shortly. When he came, there was plenty of groceries completed, so he sat down in the chair and asked, "Can I have a cup of the same tea?"

I poured him some tea and served him some cupcakes that he had purchased earlier. I sensed a bond between us. I had no idea who he was until a few months ago, and now I'm residing at his place.

"I asked him if he wanted dinner once I finished putting everything away in the cabinets."

"It would be lovely," he continued, "if you could make something simple." I was irritated with myself for asking such inane questions. I didn't want to disappoint him, despite the fact that I have no idea how to cook!

I didn't know how to make soup, so he excused himself to go to the garden for a cigarette. I wished I'd brought a cookbook with me. I was just thinking of chopping some vegetables and seasoning them with spices and a pinch of salt and pepper, along with some noodles.

When I contacted him once it was finished to see where he liked his soup, he replied he'd come to the kitchen. We ate our dinner in quiet, and his only comment was that he hadn't eaten at home in a long time.

I was too exhausted to speak, and he didn't feel safe asking me personal questions. I simply rinsed the dishes after the meal was finished, said evening, and retired to my bed.

I was relieved that I could get most of the cleaning done on the first day; thank god the shower was within the home; otherwise, I would have had to travel between the gardens!

I heard him knock on my door and asked if he might come in. He apologized for the interruption and added, "Don't you want to phone your family and let them know you're fine? It's fine with me if you keep them informed about yourself." I thanked him for the reminder, and I completely forgot to call Shaadi.

I quickly exited the room and dialed Shaadi's number; one of the servants answered and stated she was asleep; I requested her to inform that I had phoned.

Sir Malik was waiting for me when I disconnected the conversation, and he inquired whether everything was okay. I assured him not to worry because I had already passed the message that I was fine!

He thanked me once again for everything and smiled as he went to bed.

The bed was not at all comfy, but I was too weary to complain!

I awoke early the next day and decided to make breakfast. I served baguette, bacon, coffee, marmalade, butter, and fresh orange juice.

I gathered them all in the hall and placed them on a table. I heard a noise and assumed Sir was awake, so I called him and waited for a response, but there was none.

I went up to the second floor and knocked on the door. He inquired whether I required any assistance. I informed him that breakfast had been prepared.

I overheard him say he'd be ready in five minutes as I was walking out the door. When I returned to the table, I saw that the entire table had been messed up!

Bread crumbs strewn throughout the room. I was taken aback and had no idea what to say or do. I looked around the hall to see if anyone was around, but there was no one.

I wasn't expecting anyone, but I must have forgotten to latch the door and the cats were inside, so I dashed back to the kitchen and resumed my breakfast arrangements.

While preparing breakfast, I noticed him approach the kitchen and exclaimed, "Morning, I thought we were dining in the hall!"

I explained that I had failed to close the door and that cats had gone in and wrecked everything, so I had to start cooking all over again. "Please don't bother yourself; let me assist you," he remarked. "No cat could consume that much food and mess the hall so quickly." He added.

I asked him to make coffee since he wanted to help. Breakfast was ready after some time. I sat in the kitchen with the window open and we both ate a delicious breakfast.

My thoughts were preoccupied with the Cats, which spoiled my surprise.

Malik thanked me for breakfast and told that he would write down all of his appointments and emergency numbers in the notebook next to the phone if I ever needed him. Then he walked out of the house. I considered cleaning but didn't know where to begin. Sir's office and bedroom sprang to mind. I carried everything I needed for cleaning from the kitchen with me, so I didn't have to return.

I rearranged his cabinet, changed his bedsheets, and collected his filthy things for washing, before sitting on his bed, I overhearing a few individuals talking. I initially assumed there was a television on that Sir had forgotten to turn off.

I followed the sound to look for a television, but when I got to the hall, the sound stopped and there was no trace of a television. Something wasn't quite right, and I could sense it, hence I decided to stay, I should be required to stay on top of things.

I miss the days when I had to rush to catch my flight. I was thinking how difficult it is to be a housewife because I was already exhausted after only two days. Even if I take ten flights, I won't be as fatigued as I am now that the housework is done.

Because I knew Sir would not be available for lunch, I decided to prepare a meal for supper. The phone rang, and it was Jamal on the other end. Hearing his voice made me joyful.

He expressed concern for me, but primarily for his friend. I told him everything that had happened in the previous two days. He claimed Shaadi inquired as to who else was in his home, I informed him that he was absolutely alone!

We didn't get into the fight, which shocked him. When I asked Jamal to show me some of Malik's favorite foods, he laughed and said, "Now you want to find a different approach to be close to him, I see."

I burst out laughing and told him that I am willing to go to any length to make him fall in love with me! Then he presented a few items from which I could only choose those for which I already had the components in the house, and I thanked Jamal for checking on me before saying good-bye.

There was still some noise coming from the antique room, but I couldn't tell what it was. I didn't want to open the door because I was afraid there was a mouse trapped inside. If it gets away, I'll have to chase it around the house!

I dashed to the front garden, swiped it, watered the plants, then repeated the process in the back garden, before heading to the kitchen and getting to work.

Sir Malik arrived about six o'clock, but he was no longer smiling.

I noticed he was holding a newspaper and asked if I may read it; he replied yes and went upstairs; soon, he returned with a long expression and said: Didn't I tell not to touch the rooms above? After I had banned you, how could you allow yourself to do such a thing?

I explained to him that I had only cleaned and dusted, not moved anything. "You don't need to raise your voice, I'm simply standing next to you," I apologized, "sorry I did anything that upset you, we're two adults, we can converse easily without insulting one other."

Then I got up and told him, "I made dinner, it's on the table, you can serve yourself," and I went to my room with the newspaper.

I heard him dishing and transporting the meal to his room, and I was relieved that he would be eating fresh food. I wasn't like the other females who would flee his place with a single shout. I'd spent my entire life acting like a guy, so I knew how to handle one.

# Chapter 3
# Growing Up

Natural got up and went to the kitchen after reaching this point in the story; it took her a few minutes to return with two cups of tea.

She requested that I stay for lunch.

I was tempted to accept, but she became enraged and declared, "If I don't remain for lunch, it means I want to get away from her and their dull narrative!"

I simply thanked her for the offer and stated, "You have no idea how eager I am to hear the rest of the story."

"Let me tell you how I became the leader of the boy's when I was a teenager!" Natural took my hand in her and spoke.

It was a tradition among all the lads in my day that whoever was bold and brave might be the group leader.

Since the father of one of our neighbors died, we determined that whoever could stay in his coffin in the church for one hour before being buried may be the leader, and that this should take place at night rather than during the day!

We were a group of eight, including me, but five of us gave up, leaving only two of us. We arrived at a well-known church at 12 a.m.; I knew where the body was kept and invited the other two to join us; however, they were startled and fled when they heard a commotion.

I stepped inside and was able to fit into his coffin. I was not terrified of the body and stayed there for an hour.

After I found my way out, I noticed that everyone was clapping for me. I've been their leader since that day! If there was a conflict, they expected me to intervene and put an end to it. If they had a disagreement or a problem, I was the one who had to make the decisions and find solutions to their problems.

I attempted to mind my own business after what happened with Sir Malik; it was our first argument, and I didn't want to put both of us in a difficult situation.

I began working in the garden by cleaning the tiny pool, replacing damaged pots with new ones, chopping away at unsightly branches, and eventually watering the plants. I didn't want to go inside because the weather was wonderful, and I was having a great time outside.

I didn't bother to keep the breakfast ready because I assumed Sir was not at home. I was startled to hear a door open. I dashed into the kitchen and took refuge there. I didn't want to look him in the eyes.

Natural took a short break from the story and remarked, "I reminisced about being the head of a boy's group and how fearless I was. Now see, I was so afraid of Sir that I ended up hiding in the kitchen; it's amazing how love can change you!"

I overheard a man debating doctor appointments while I was there. I sat on the ground because I didn't want to be seen, but I knew there were more than one. Who could they possibly be? I wondered. How did they get in without my knowledge?

They went silent quickly, and I assumed they had already left until I heard the hall door open. When I came out of the kitchen, Malik was staring at the pool, and saw me, he remarked, "Good morning, or should I say good afternoon," I responded, and he went on to remark, "I have never seen the pool that clean in my life, how did you do it? It had to have taken a lot of effort!"

"Actually, it was the water that was dirty, not the pool, so I just tossed it away, washed the walls, and poured fresh water," I said.

He was so taken aback by my work that he began to admire the rest of the garden as well. I didn't want to get in the way, so I didn't inquire about his companions who had just arrived. I assumed he would have told me without my asking if he wanted me to know. I avoided interfering as much as possible.

He then asked if I could make him a cup of tea, since he enjoys drinking it while sitting by the pool. He was off to his meetings after his tea. I considered taking a stroll and doing some little shopping.

I walked all over that neighborhood, and when I returned, I noticed Jamal waiting for me in his car in front of the house! I greeted him and apologized for not being able to invite him in because I wasn't sure how Malik would react if I brought someone into the house without his knowledge!

"Don't worry about these things, I just want to know how things are going with you," he added. "Shaadi was concerned, which is why she requested me to come here." He attracted her interest, and she was eager to learn more about him! She's hoping he hasn't picked up on your identity yet.

I told him not to worry and that I had gotten into an argument with Sir, he chuckled and said, "So, you had your first fight with your love."

"He came into my office yesterday and showed me the newspaper where your picture was published, and he wanted me to explain why a pilot was working as a housemaid at his home! However, the explanation I provided didn't satisfy him, therefore I believe he wants to find out more about you!"

I became concerned and inquired, "What did you say, Jamal? I hope you didn't tell him the truth."

"He is my friend, and it is tough to lie to him," he said with a smile, "but I have promised you, so I won't say anything until you want me to."

I didn't tell Jamal about the visitors since I didn't want to bother him. I was afraid he'd think I was a loud lady attempting to maintain control from now on, so I apologized and said, "I need to go back in before Malik arrives, or we'll both be caught!" Then we said our goodbyes.

I decided to make supper, and when I was finished in the kitchen, I served myself and returned to my room, leaving his part on the hall dining table. I didn't want to look him in the eyes. I'm not sure why, but I was afraid that if he asked me about the truth, I wouldn't be able to lie to him again, and everything would change. He wasn't yet ready to learn who I was or why I was there!

Jamal assured me he'll keep playing until no one is wounded, and if one of us gets hurt, he'll intervene and call a halt to the game. Why did he act as if this was a game or that one of us should be injured?

He knocked on the door and asked if I might join him for supper because he dislikes eating alone! It's fine with me, I stated.

I opened the door to give him my answer, but he was already sitting at the table and waiting for me. He wanted to know if I made his favorite cuisine by accidentally or if Jamal told him. I informed him that I had enquired of him.

He then proceeded while eating his food, saying, "I assumed you'd leave!"

I informed him that he had not yet terminated my employment and that I would continue to work. "I never fired anyone; they all departed on their own," he said.

I looked him in the eyes and told him, "I am unusual." "Yes, you are entirely different, you are Pilot housemaid!" he said, as if he was expecting me to say.

He was expecting a reaction from me now that he knew my secret, but I remained calm and said nothing. "What do you want to know about me?" he said again. "Why did you choose me to finish your experience instead of others?"

As I previously stated, I wanted to try something new, get away from my profession, and learn how to do housekeeping. Jamal offered your home because he stated you are a gentleman and that I would be secure there. You're also on the lookout for a maid.

I questioned him why he was attempting to come up with a new reason to get rid of me. "Is there anything wrong with what I've done so far?"

He claimed everything was fine and that he liked the way I worked, but that he couldn't offer me a high income like I was making as a pilot.

I informed him that I had never expected a payment while he was providing me with a place to sleep and food, which was more than enough to meet all of my expenses.

He also requested that I refrain from entering his room or workplace. He stated that he likes things the way they are and that finding what he wants is much easier. That made perfect sense after he explained it to me, and I promised him that I would not enter any of those rooms without his permission.

We completed supper, and I offered him tea, which he eagerly accepted. I could see he was struggling to keep himself from asking me a question! I was scrubbing the table, and he was assisting me as well.

I wanted to go to the kitchen to fetch the tea, but he insisted on keeping me. He will be the one responsible for it.

That night, Sir Malik was particularly attractive. I knew he was feeling the same way because of the way he looked at me, but I didn't want to rush anything and urged myself to be tough!

He handed me a cup of tea and said, "Natural, I'd like you to assist me in getting to know you better?" I'd like to learn more about you!

At that moment, all I wanted to do was rise up and dance or hold him so tightly! I was expecting him to find a way to get to know me, and here he was, sitting in front of me like a nice kid, eager to learn about me!

I told him all he wanted to know about me, including my background, parents, character, and Shaadi. He was simply paying attention to me in the same way that the therapist was paying attention to his patient! He looked happier and more comfortable after learning about my history.

He took my hand in his and said, "I'm sorry for what happened to your parents; sure, you had a hard time adjusting to reality as a child, but I'm incredibly proud of who you've become now. When do you think you'll be back at work?"

"In a few weeks," I told him. He stated that until then, he will enjoy having me in his place. Finally, he walked me to my room and then went to his.

Oh my God, what a night I had, it was so lovely, he had a whole new face and attitude, and I wanted Shaadi and Jamal were here to see Malik's transformation. I sensed a bond between us, and I'm sure he did as well.

# Chapter 4
# Incomplete Introduction

I was fatigued but didn't want to stop Natural. When I looked at Natural's face, it appeared that she had already traveled back in time, and she was saying:

That day, I awoke early. I was feeling energized, and the garden wasn't big enough for me to begin my run, so I went to the park. It was the end of the autumn season, and winter was approaching. Park appeared to be spectacular.

Sir was already awake when I returned; he appeared concerned and approached me, asking, "Thought you had left without saying goodbye!"

I smiled and said, "Good morning!" I'm not going anywhere until you tell me to, I informed him, since I need to stay in shape, and I used to go for a daily run. If I didn't notify you, please accept my apologies. I immediately washed and went to the kitchen.

I noticed him reading a newspaper, and he handed it to me with the request that I read the first page.

I was not interested in reading the entire tale because there was a picture of a young couple who died in a vehicle accident. Every day, I read of people who have died in car accidents as a result of driving too fast or while inebriated!

Our youth, unfortunately, do not take things seriously and always end up causing harm to themselves and others. I spoke.

"Both were my students, in love, and preparing to marry!" he replied. "I used to give them a private lesson at my home. I haven't heard anything from them in a few months, until I saw the news today. They were three of them, two ladies and a male from the same class.

"Jamal contacted me in the evening, I still remember it. He'd been in an accident, and his car was badly damaged, and he needed me to come pick him up the same night.

"Two of them arrived early for class, and the third was scheduled as well, but she didn't. I assume she was sick, so she didn't show up. I'm referring to Natasha, who was killed in a vehicle accident. I told them they could continue painting without me, and I'd be back in an hour."

For private lessons, I usually let students arrive early and practice for as long as they desired. I used to let them use one of the ancient objects in the room as a model and create a tale around it. Three of them were truly exceptional performers.

When I returned that night, there was no one there.

After speaking about his students, Sir Malik looked a little woozy.

He claimed it was his migraine, and once he gets agitated, it really starts bothering him, so I rose up to help him. I simply offered him a glass of water.

I wanted to do something to lift Sir Malik's spirits, so I asked him if he enjoyed playing football after lunch. "Can you actually play football?" he asked, looking at my face.

I burst out laughing and said to him, "Why do you think I'm teasing you? Please just go to market and grab a ball. I'll show you what I can do with that ball after lunch!"

He accepted right away and went to the nearest grocery after lunch, returning with a ball in his hand. He was like a ten-year-old youngster who was looking forward to playing the best football game with his friend.

He inquired as to how I wished to begin. I instructed him to begin dribble first, and then we'd see who could keep the ball for the longest! He could dribble for ten seconds before passing the ball to me and standing there watching me.

I dribbled nonstop for five minutes, and when I stopped, his countenance was so amusing and full of astonishment. Then we played for an hour, and none of us realized it! "I need a squad to win you," Malik stated as he halted a game. "I have never seen someone play this brilliantly in my life!" His expression was quite amusing.

It was the first time I'd ever worn my hair down. When he saw my long hair, I noticed how his eyes widened. "Natural, you are quite attractive, and your name corresponds to your attractiveness," he said.

I was proud of my beauty at the moment. As a result, I expressed my gratitude to him.

I went to the kitchen to cook a meal while Sir had a shower. Malik hadn't left the house all day and had spent time with me, which was incredible; he was walking over to me and didn't even realize it! I wish Jamal could have been here to witness all of this.

Shaadi called that night, moaning that I hadn't gone home since I'd left, and that Prince Albert was coming for a visit next week, and she was sure he'd start looking for me, so I should take a leave and join her before he finds out why I'd gone AWOL!

I was so irritated with Shaadi, I informed her that he now has a wife, so what does he want from me? Shaadi, on the other hand, was adamant that I be present when he arrived, no matter what. I accepted since I realized I didn't have a choice.

I honestly couldn't sleep after Shaadi's call. Malik was making an effort to get to know me, and I was ecstatic with his development. I'm sure if he finds out about Albert and his proposal, it would hurt his feelings, and there won't be enough time for me to demonstrate to him that there was nothing between us.

Shaadi continued repeating that we were too dissimilar people from two separate cultures and communities, with the exception of our shared language! I'm sure she's expecting me to run up to her and cry and tell her she's correct.

My feelings for Malik are genuine, and I was doing everything I could to help him. I wish I could have been like any other girl and simply looked him in the eyes and told him that I love him, and then left it at that, but I lacked the guts, and as I previously stated, I never learned.

I was buried in my thoughts when I heard a loud scream. I leapt from my bed and dashed to the door, only to find it locked. I started hammering on the door and attempting to pull the handle to my side, but it appeared that someone on the other side was holding it!

When I went to open the window, I saw a woman on fire, screaming and fleeing toward the pool, where she immediately dived in. I was able to open the window, crawled out, and proceeded to assist her.

She was terribly burned when I dragged her from the pool! Sir requested that I leave an old sofa in the front lawn until he finds a family to whom he may gift it.

So I kept her on a three-seater sofa while I walked inside to get my towel. I asked her who she was and what she was doing here once I had dried her.

She attempted to communicate with me through sign language. I discovered she is deaf! Fortunately, I understood sign language because one of the boys in my group was deaf and taught me when I was a teenager.

She wanted to tell me about the incident while holding my arm, but something was stopping her! I explained how she arrived at the house. Due to her injuries, she was unable to communicate. When I asked her about the fire, she burst into tears, causing her wounds to bleed!

I told her I'd take her inside so I could assist her...

# Chapter 5
# Woken or Asleep

I sat on the bed and opened my eyes to see Malik shaking me. He felt my forehead and asked if I was ok as I was warm!

It was almost time for lunch. He was concerned and expressed regret for entering my room without permission. He assumed I had locked myself in the room and only managed to access it after fumbling with the door handle.

"Have you attempted to exit through the window? Broken glass has scratched all of your hands!"

I just didn't know how to react to his questions, so I looked around the room, convinced I was having a nightmare. I apologized to Sir Malik and explained that I had a dreadful dream that lasted for a long time!

He requested that I go take a shower in order to feel more refreshed. I dashed into the bathroom and washed up right away. I was irritated that I had slept too much.

After that, I headed straight to the kitchen. I could see Sir Malik approaching, so I pretended I didn't see him. I didn't want to tell him about my dream because I was afraid of how he would react after hearing the complete tale.

Sir Malik remarked, "Don't cook anything today; I'll get food from outside," and I asked Jamal to lunch.

Sir went to open the gate after the doorbell rang. I thanked him. Jamal entered holding a large watermelon.

We gave him a warm welcome and invited him to tea in the garden. He looked at me and asked, "Natural, are you all, right?" You didn't appear to be having a good night's sleep.

"I heard her chatting in her dreams, so I knew something was wrong, therefore I planned to wake her up, and today, I won't let her work at all; I will be at her side," Malik continued.

I understood what that look meant when Jamal blinked at me. We shared a grin. Sir Malik went outside and ordered lunch. I considered going to my room and relaxing while Jamal and Malik were busy talking politics and business.

I came out shortly after hearing my name. Jamal inquired as to what time I would be ready in the morning so that the driver could arrive!

Sir Malik's face was irritated, so asked whether I was leaving tomorrow. In my place, Jamal responded, "Natural and her aunt are hosting a special guest, Prince Albert!" As a mark of respect for the royal family, she must be present.

I didn't want Jamal to be the one to deliver the news, but he didn't allow me the opportunity to explain myself. Sir Malik was no longer interested in looking at me.

"I told both of them about Prince Albert, which Shaadi had told me about, just last night. I haven't decided on a time or anything else yet; I'll phone Shaadi and let her know." I answered him.

After a while, Jamal thanked us for the dinner and walked away, apologizing if he had caused any inconvenience. I assured him that it was fine and that I would take care of it.

I began cleaning, with Malik's assistance; however, I dropped a teacup on the ground, which broke; both of us bent at the same time to pick up the broken pieces; nevertheless, I cut my finger on the sharp edge of a cup; he let me to sit on the sofa, and then brought a plaster to stop the bleeding!

We had no words, only heat between us! I let him look after me because he was so near to me that I could count his heartbeats!

He had my hand in his and was pulling my hair away from my face with his other hand! When the phone rang, I was sure he was going to kiss me. I hoped he never had a phone in his house because he jumped up and apologized to go grab it!

What a moment it was, I was sitting motionless, waiting for a kiss! I wanted him to hold me, to gaze into his eyes and release all that energy, to tell him I was dying for his love! But I guess it wasn't the right time!

He took the phone, returned quickly, and stated that he had a lesson that he needed to attend!

I explained to him that Shaadi is the only family member I have, and I must obey her orders. I'll go early tomorrow and return later that evening.

He informed me that I arrived of my own free choice and that I could go wherever I wanted; he would never stop me! He expressed surprise that Jamal was also aware of the situation, given that he was the last to be briefed.

When the guy you love said something like this, it was a little uncomfortable! I was expecting him to say something like, "Natural, don't go," or "Let me give you a ride," or "Call me from there and explain to me about everything," but instead he just let me go!

The plot was then paused till this point. Natural motioned for me to take a seat at the table before going into the kitchen to prepare lunch, or rather, early dinner. Sir Malik had been left alone in the house, so it was just the two of us.

We sat at the pool after she poured a delightful Turkish coffee, and she continued: That night, I was not in the mood to pack anything. I sat bedside bed and said my prayers before going to sleep.

I had an ache in my right arm, so I folded my sleeve up and examined it; there were numerous scratches, and I couldn't recall when I had harmed myself.

Meanwhile, I heard a horrific scream, identical to last night's, but this time coming from the next room!

Fortunately, my door was not locked this time, so I stepped outside and followed the voice, which came from the antique room that Sir had previously forbade me from entering!

When I opened it, I observed a young man attempting to defraud a woman. I tried to push my way in, but the door slammed shut in my face, preventing me from going inside. The girl was the same one who had been burned the night before!

I couldn't get through the door as I couldn't open it. I dashed upstairs to wake Malik, but he was fast asleep. I shook his feet several times, but he didn't stir. I returned and tried the door again; this time it opened easily, and I saw her sitting on the bed, crying and alone. She appeared to be terrified, and I felt the same way. I couldn't decide whether or not to approach her.

I felt a hand on my shoulder and turned around to see Sir Malik... Why was I in the antique room, he inquired? or if he can assist me in locating it! Why was I attempting to raise him?

I didn't want to inform Malik I was sleep walking because it was so early in the morning. I informed him there were some noises coming from the room, and that I assumed it was a rat, and that I had come to inform him before they chewed anything.

My body was shivering, I pretended nothing was wrong I told him, let's keep a trap for it and came out of the room.

I pretended nothing was wrong despite the fact that my body was shivering. I exited the room after telling him, "Let's keep a trap for it."

I apologized once more. I came up to ask for permission, but he was still asleep!

"No problem, sweetie, you are always welcome to my bedroom," he responded with a smile. We both chuckled after that.

I walked to my room and closed the door behind. What was going on with me? I was too afraid to tell him about my visions because it was so terrifying.

Malik was preparing breakfast in the kitchen as I hurriedly dressed and contacted my aunt to arrange a driver. Malik said he could borrow Jamal's car to pick me up if I needed it. I promised him I'd call him once Shaadi's formalities were through.

I could tell Malik was planning to ask me something, so I decided to be the one to assist him this time. "Do you have any questions for me before I go?"

"Is there any history between you and Prince?" he inquired.

I was overjoyed to be able to respond to that question; I told him NEVER, but he proposed to me once, I declined, he returned home, married a princess, and that was the whole of our relationship.

"My aunt is a successful businesswoman who is also active in politics, but when it comes to money, she rarely says no... Albert attempted everything he could to acquire me, but he was unsuccessful." He even assumed I was transgender! He couldn't deal with me because I was too complicated!

Malik said, "Me too, until I learned out what you're interested in, I was thinking you weren't straight!"

When the doorbell rang, I knew it was time to leave; I wanted to hug him and tell him to wait for me, "Darling, I'll be back, Don't worry, I'm all yours and more." But I couldn't, so all I got was a handshake and a farewell.

# Chapter 6
# Solitary Party Hall

Everyone was preoccupied with preparing for Prince Albert's arrival, but Shaadi was waiting for me, hugging me and admitting that she was lonely without me.

That was amusing because I had been away from home for so long, studying and practicing at the camp. She has never expressed her want to see me!

She inquired about Sir Malik! I informed her that he is a respected man with strong self-control, and that he already knows who I am.

I'm not sure why Shaadi was pleased to hear that.

She showed me to my room, where all of the decorations had been altered, including attractive blinds and the most recent model sofa; my bed was no longer for one person, and I believe the entire family could fit in it.

Why were there so many changes, I inquired? As a pilot, she replied, my room should reflect my profession and individuality; very soon, people will be concerned about where I live and what style I choose!

I reminded her that more than half of the people in this country can't afford a meal at their table, if there is one! You'd like me to show them this. Come on, where has your compassion gone? I will never promote this way of living to anyone; all I want is to live a simple life like everyone else.

"Right now, you are coming from that needy author's place, he has hypnotized you," Shaadi added, giving me one of those odd looks. "After a few days here, you'll be back to your old self."

I knew that disputing with her would be pointless, so I decided not to say anything. She handed me a pricey gown and told me it was for the ball tonight, and that the hairdresser will be in my room to assist me in getting ready.

"What would you have done if you were in my place at that point, Yalda?" Natural said, putting an end to her story. '

"There wasn't much of a choice, to be honest." I informed her.

"Bravo," she murmured as she clapped her palm.

Then she went on to say, "I was entirely confused; on the one hand, I was in love with someone with whom I couldn't be honest and tell him the truth; on the other hand, Shaadi was attempting to set me up with his clients in order to generate more business for herself!" Worst of all, my visions!

I don't know who I could talk to about it. I wanted some assistance to figure out why I was getting those dreams over and over again.

It didn't take long for me to get ready; nevertheless, I didn't wear the outfit that Shaadi had chosen for me... I simply wore a regular suit with my hair open.

There was only Shaadi and Albert in the ballroom when I arrived; there was no trace of the ballroom or other guests. Albert was not shocked but Shaadi was irritated to see me in such clothing!

I shook his hand, and he proceeded to ask me a series of questions, including how many trips I had taken and what I had been up to. I detailed my courses to him, but when I got to the part about Sir Malik, Shaadi shifted the subject. She did not want me to go any farther.

"She was busy with various functions, couldn't join, maybe next time," he explained when I inquired why he didn't bring his wife. He responds.

I couldn't understand why Shaadi had to go to such lengths to enjoy Albert's presence when the food on the table could feed a hundred people!

Albert invited me to join him for a walk after supper, which I accepted. We walked around the entire garden. He handed me one of his cigars while we were walking; I thanked him and took one.

Then he revealed that he couldn't stop thinking about me. He assumed he'd forget about me after marriage, but it got worse, and he started missing me more! He claimed that I was the only lady he could never have, and that with the position he currently holds, he could get anyone he wanted!

He claimed to have made a deal with Shaadi to get me out of that house. He was also aware of my feelings toward Sir Malik.it appeared that Shaadi had been reporting to him all along! I advised him to concentrate on his wife and spend time with her rather than following me.

Then he gave me a horrible laugh and said, "His father-in-law owns a lot of gold mines and gas pipelines, not to mention a lot of other assets and stuff all over the world, so I had done what my father wanted me to do, it was all socially constructed."

He was sad to the point of suicidal ideation! To be honest, I felt awful for him at the time, but I didn't want to offer him kindness since I knew he'd exploit it. He was confused as to why I was chasing Sir Malik when he was right in front of me, promising me all!

He promised to stay devoted to me and keep our relationship hidden from the rest of the world!

He tried to stop me in the Maize by pulling my hand towards himself and kissing me with the other hand around my waist. I struck his face and he fell to the ground!

I attempted to grab his hand because his nose was bleeding, but he said no! You have forgotten that I grew up with boys, I told him!

He stated that these are the things that make him want me even more, and that he would not give up until he receives what he desires! He went away after that!

I just sat on the ground, irritated by my actions, and wished my parents were with me at the time! I needed their love and assistance because I was so lonely.

I rested my eyes for a moment and had another dream in which I was sinking and the same girl from my prior nightmares was attempting to save me!

I was dragged from the water by her! I could see her face well this time, and there were no burned marks on her face. I thanked her and asked her name, to which she replied in hand signals that she was not permitted to tell me any!

When I turned to see where I was, I noticed Albert sprinting towards me.

She was gone again. Albert sat down next to me and inquired, "Why did you jump into the pool wearing your clothes?" At the very least, he could've assisted me in removing them!

"It just came up after I punched you in the face," I said.

He assisted me in standing up, but I was wearing a towel and asked him who had given it to me. Obviously, one of the servants replied!

I rose up and walked inside, Shaadi was so shocked to find me wet that she nearly yelled! "How did this happen? Why are you soaked? What's causing Albert's nose to bleed? Have you two gotten into a conflict?"

"We wanted to have a run around the Maze," Albert explained this time, "but she ended up in the water, and I got bashed by the tree! Don't worry, it was all in great fun! We both had a good time." Then we both laughed!

I returned to my room, but I had no idea what had happened; something didn't feel right.

I got up early the next day for my walk. I was relieved that no one was gazing at me as I ran, unlike the park adjacent to Sir's house.

Albert and I had a full day of activities planned by Shaadi! We went horse riding after breakfast, but Albert was not communicating with me; after all, I owed him an apology!

I stopped, assisted him in dismounting, shook his hand, and regretted the previous night!

"The only way I can forgive you is if you kiss me," he murmured, refusing to let go of my hand. Obviously, I wasn't the one to say yes to his request, so I informed him that if he still had his private jet, I could fly him to my wonderland!

I was missing the blue sky, so I decided to fly for at least a few hours! He became delighted and requested that one of his men ready his jet.

Shaadi had an island not far from her palace, which she referred to as the 'greatest gift ever!' We both made it to the plane, along with two servants. My aunt was insistent about not coming; I believe she wished to produce a romantic atmosphere for us!

We were there for 30 minutes, and I felt completely different after flying that baby; I felt like I was still useful! Albert was unimpressed, and he inquired as to what was so unique about this location, given that they own many of them!

I requested that he join me... We went for a while and came upon a lake with sweet water and the most gorgeous pink dolphins in the middle of the island!

He was overwhelmed by the beauty! I told him to go to the water and see what they'd do. He was afraid, but stood there and watched me dive and dance with them!

Then he went into the lake and began playing with dolphins. We were so preoccupied that we didn't notice it was growing dark, so we immediately changed. "Thank you for sharing the magnificent Dreamland with me," Albert murmured as he kissed my forehead before I started the engine.

I told him that he is the first to learn about this location, and that even Shaadi is unaware of the dolphins! He wanted to know whether Malik knew anything about the place. NO, I replied. He clapped his hands and tanked me once again.

Shaadi was eagerly awaiting our arrival. She was overjoyed that I had made Albert smile. I returned to my room to recover after dinner. I was exhausted, so I went to bed after a shower. It was already morning when I opened my eyes!

I just dressed in a white gown and drank a cup of coffee in my room before going to church with Shaadi. She urged me to stop chasing Malik on the way back so that I could get a closer look at Albert and the future that I would have by being beside him.

I informed her that he is a married man who already has someone in his life, and that just help him reconnect with his wife rather than creating distance between them.

"We are not the ones who have extended him an invitation to attend; if his wife truly cared, she would have called at least once to find out where her husband is, or Albert could have called to check on his wife," Shaadi added, chuckling.

Albert's life is a complete disaster, and now is the opportunity to take advantage of it! This is our moment; it is preferable for you to put your emotions aside and begin building your own path, one that will make you one of the most powerful women in the world! Consider what we could achieve with my wealth, your skill, and Albert's influence!

I requested that the driver come to a complete halt since I couldn't stand it any longer. When Shaadi summoned me back to the car, I informed her that just because she had raised and cared for me didn't mean she could speak for me.

Albert is like a buddy to me, and he needs someone to be by his side that he has never had. He needed us as friends. I can be his best loyal companion, but I'll never be his lover!

I've always loved one person and will continue to do so no matter what happens in the future.

I could have claimed you are a ruthless woman if I didn't know you Shaadi or anything about your history and love tale. Why are you advising me to take the incorrect route when you've been in a similar situation before?

My parents could not be saved by your money or your status! Open your eyes to the reality, how much are you gathering properties, money, gold, products, and so on? They haven't and never will recover the anguish of the past for you!

"My father did you a tremendous injustice by refusing to let you be with the one you loved! That doesn't imply you should treat me the same way! I still like and respect everything you've done for me, but when it comes to my life, I'd rather make my own decisions!" I informed her.

I made a mistake by abandoning Malik and arriving here. Even though I knew you were wrong, I wanted to please you.'

I'm sorry, but I'm not able to continue this filthy game. Albert is someone I care about, yet selling myself to make him happy is the wrong approach to keep someone happy. If you truly care, don't be the one who gives him pleasure for the night only to kick him out the next day!

"We just came out of the Church, praying for forgiveness, health, and happiness," I added. Which one do you wish to accomplish in your life? All of this money isn't going to help us in the next world, so why spend our lives chasing it only to keep it and live another life?

Shaadi was listening to what I was saying and remained completely silent. I believe she wished for someone to tell her the truth and burst her bubble. I didn't return to Albert to say my goodbyes. I put on a hat and returned to Sir Malik's mansion.

Natural was in tears as she got to this section of the narrative. I considered changing the subject and asked her if we could take a walk through their garden and if she could show me some of Sir Malik's works of art. She was delighted to oblige. My father arrived later that evening to pick me up.

I assured Natural that I would return the next day to hear the rest of the story. I was quiet on the drive to the hotel. My father was aware that something was awry, but he didn't want to bother me!

# Chapter 7
# Grab the Opportunity

I was so eager the next day that I requested my father to drop me off at Sir Malik's residence as soon as he could. He told me to stay calm as it was inappropriate to disturb them so early in the morning.

Sir Malik insisted that my father join him for coffee this time, so they both sat on the front garden bench and started chatting out about climate, governance, smog, and other topics!

Natural was in the kitchen preparing a meal. I said my goodbyes to my father and asked Sir for permission to go to Natural. Sir Malik told my father that he would give me a ride this time, and we both appreciated him.

Natural, I assumed, was making lunch.

We talked for a while before she joined me and we both sat out this time: After I left my aunt that day, I went straight to Malik's house, didn't have the key, and hoped he was at home. I didn't even have money to pay taxi.

Sir was home, and he was not pleased to see me there. I inquired whether he could pay the driver.

We entered once he had paid. I walked straight to my room to change, and when I returned, he was sitting on the sofa, pretending to read the newspaper!

I was just gone for half a day, and now I'm back after two! I gave him full permission to be irritated! I took a step forward and expressed my regret for arriving late.

He expressed concern and asked why I hadn't called and informed him that I would be staying longer. He had been at home for the past two days since I had forgotten to take my extra keys.

I felt embarrassed since I couldn't think of anything to say.

I looked into his frightened eyes and said, "I know what I did was entirely wrong; I apologize; I will make sure it does not happen again." Then he shook his head, and I realized it was his migraine, which he had told me about before, and which he gets whenever he is anxious.

Sir got ready to leave and said he'd be back for dinner as I started cleaning the house. I assumed he missed my meals.

I went to the kitchen after I had finished cleaning the house. I was also cleaning up the garden while the supper was being prepared.

Soon after, the lunch was ready, and I returned to the house, where I spotted blood spots all over the floor, which I followed to the bathroom!

I heard someone while trying to open the door. I was a little concerned, but I decided to push the door open, which it did without difficulty.

I was expecting to see the same person in the bathtub, so I went to the front and inquired, "What was the blood for?" I couldn't tell what she was carrying in her arm because I couldn't see it, but I could hear her humming!

Out of nowhere, I heard Malik calling my name, and asked the girl to stay here until I came back! But I knew it was a silly request!

Sir was wondering why there were blood drops on the ground. He asked me When I heard Malik shouting my name, I told the girl to wait for me! But I was well aware that this was a ridiculous request! Sir was perplexed as to why there were blood splattered throughout the floor. He inquired as to whether or not I had been wounded. The rough edge of the broken glass had injured my foot when I claimed there was a glass on the floor! What a liar I'd turned into, I thought to myself.

I refused to show him the wound because I didn't have one! He motioned for me to take a seat on the sofa while he dashed upstairs to get some Band-Aids and gauze, as well as his safety box. I knew she was gone if I went to the bathroom as usual.

He walked down the stairs and sat in front of my seat on the ground.

I told him it was no big thing and he grabbed my ankle and said, "I think this is a major deal!"

I have been going around the home with a piece of glass trapped in my left ankle! However, when and how did I injure myself? I was already cleaning the house and heading to the kitchen, My gut told me it was her; she was the one behind everything! That young lady was a snob.

Malik yelled my name and asked, "Natural, are you all, right?" I have to take you to the hospital because I can't get the broken glass out of your ankle! That is something that only an expert can do!

I was still stunned, However I agreed with him, and he phoned a taxi and assisted me in boarding.

There was a hospital nearby, so we went to the emergency room, where the glass was quickly removed with the help of nurses and doctors, and I ended up with 10 stitches. After three hours, we returned home. I told him I had already prepared dinner since we were both starving.

Dinner was served in the garden. He was putting food on the table for both of us. I was astounded by how concerned he was.

He said that it was his fault that the tea cups were left on the ground. I informed him that I was the one who had been so irresponsible, and that is why, while working, I needed to open my eyes wider!

He was hungry, so he double-served himself and ate everything. It's a good sensation to see people you care about eating the cuisine you prepared with passion.

I went to my room after dinner with his support. He asked whether I wanted him to stay, and I said No so he went to his bed. I fell asleep very immediately because of all the painkillers they gave me in the hospital.

Sir stayed at home to watch me for five days while my wound recovered. We were approaching Christmas, and I was nearing the conclusion of my time with Sir.

Jamal called to invite Malik to a Christmas party one day. He also notified Prince Albert and his wife that they would be in attendance.

Shaadi wasn't calling herself since she was still furious with me. I invited Sir to come, and he agreed, but he explained that he is only coming because of me; otherwise, he does not attend these types of large gatherings and festivities. I made the decision to go early in the morning and assist with the preparations.

I bid Sir farewell and informed him that I would see him at the Party. Shaadi was not in attendance. When I returned to my room, I saw that she had procured another gorgeous ball gown for me.

My wound had entirely healed, and I was able to walk without difficulty.

I felt strange, so I sat down on my bed for a moment, looked around, and wondered why my aunt would host such a large party and invite Sir Malik while also inviting Albert.

Was she looking forward to a conflict on Christmas Eve? She had to be up to something, didn't she? However, I was unable to decipher her thoughts.

I knew something was wrong with me after what happened that day at Sir's house and I ended myself in the hospital.

"Nowadays, everyone goes to a psychologist or any therapist to chat and ask for help," Natural added, "whereas previously, only crazy individuals or those with major troubles were sent."

She went on to say, "I had no idea Prince Albert was staying with his wife in one of the Shaadi's palace's largest guest apartments." In the garden, I noticed them walking together. I was relieved to discover Albert had finally begun to love and settle down with his wife.

Even though the sun was sinking, the celebration had already begun. It was my first time dressing up and appearing in front of Malik. I chose one of my mother's gowns. It was

Christmas eve the last time she wore it, yet I still remember it…

I wore open hair and high-heeled sandals! I was pleased with my appearance and relieved that I was not overdressed! Still no word from Shaadi, and I knew she was waiting for me to apologize to her!

I made up my mind to see her. I had never been permitted into her room before and had no idea how it looked! I knocked on the door, and she let me in since she mistook me for one of her servants, yet she was seated in front of her dressing table.

I greeted hello, and she responded by turning to face me. I hugged her and apologized for not calling and checking up on her for so long! However, just because I acknowledged my presence does not imply that my beliefs have changed!

She was taken aback when she saw me in my mother's outfit and said, "You look gorgeous tonight!" She then asked, "Let's not spoil tonight's delight with toxic thoughts!"

I wasn't sure about the toxic thoughts, but I agreed with her and didn't want any DISCUSSION! So, we started heading towards the main hall together.

I noticed Albert standing next to the window, he moved forward and greeted me, then began asking how I was or how I spent my days and nights without him, I began to chuckle, then I noticed his wife approaching us.

She was a lovely lady, and we were introduced, but Albert then left us there and fled! He must have wanted to watch how we reacted or how we got along!

She inquired as to how long we had known each other, and before I could respond, she inquired again: was it before or after he married?

I told her before he married, and just for a short time! He's more like a buddy.

I sensed she had more questions, and I tried to flee, but she caught me and asked, "Are you really a first lady pilot?" "I don't know if I'm the first, but yes, I'm a pilot," I responded with a smile. But there was something she said that night that really upset me.

So this is how I fool and trap the guys: I dress up, attempt to show off that I'm a pilot, then tell them about my parents' tragedy and seek for empathy!

I knew she was jealous, which was fine because it showed she cared about Albert. I took her hand in mine and said, "Let's not ruin tonight's party," then excused myself and walked away.

Albert, I noticed, was keeping an eye on us. I felt relieved that I had done the right thing by refusing to give her what she desired.

I was becoming concerned as the sun set and there was still no sight of Sir Malik and Jamal. I even tried calling him on his landline, but he didn't answer.

One by one, visitors arrived, all eager to see Prince Albert and his wife. Almost all of them were my aunt's business associates and country's wealthiest people!

Malik and Jamal showed up at 8:00 p.m., I believe.

Apparently, Jamal was fine because this was not his first time, but Sir Malik was clearly unhappy from the start. I went up to the front and greeted them before leading them to their table.

For the first minute, Malik was adoring me, but then Jamal yelled his name and shouted, "You're swallowing her with your eyes man!"

I pretended not to hear anything, but I was ecstatic that I had managed to capture his attention. I requested the volunteers to bring them some non-alcoholic beverages.

My entire duty that night was to keep Malik pleased so he wouldn't feel left out.

As if it were their home and kingdom, Prince Albert and his wife went around to each table and greeted everyone. When he arrived at Sir Malik and Jamal's table, he declined to shake Malik's hand and quickly left. It was incredibly weird, and I'm sure everyone noticed!

I expected him to be more gentlemanly and respect him, but he refused. Albert's eyes shone with jealousy.

I invited Malik and Jamal to follow me after dinner so I could show them about my aunt's palace, but Malik was not in a good mood and stated it wouldn't be proper for two guys and a lady to leave the hall; I accepted his opinion but wanted to assist him for a little to get away from the crowd.

He was still irritated by Albert's actions, I knew.

The biggest error I made that night was seeing Albert pointing at me and telling me to follow him outdoors surreptitiously.

I was completely unaware that Malik was keeping an eye on us the entire time. Albert was waiting for me on the next balcony, clutching a jewelry box. I inquired as to what was so pressing that he needed to meet in secret. responded:

"As a thank you for the last time we traveled to your paradise together, I purchased you a diamond necklace!" I informed him that we are simply friends, and that I am always by his side as a friend, and that what I did was take a break for both of us!

I accepted the present since he insisted on having it. Meanwhile, Sir Malik was looking for a smoking space, and the assistance had led him to the same location where we were, where they had inadvertently overheard our talk and returned inside.

I dashed upstairs and tucked the gift box away in my room. I returned to the hall and discovered they were nowhere to be seen! When I questioned what had happened, everyone at their table stated they had left. While I was seeking for them, Shaadi flashed me a misleading smile!

"What happened, why did they leave without saying goodbye?" I said as I approached her, she appeared to be busy. She said, "Sir Malik planned to leave soon, and Jamal, I assume, followed him; they were looking for you, but I assured them I'd offer them my compliments."

I was furious with myself for abandoning them to go to Albert. I had no idea what had occurred, but I assumed they were bored.

That night, the party carried on until two o'clock, I was fatigued, and Shaadi introduced me to a slew of bachelor guys.

Every Christmas eve, it was customary for the young couples to have the first dance, and Prince Albert and his wife were the ones who liked it the most. The remainder of the party didn't annoy me at all.

I changed and went to bed as soon as half of the people had left. I spent the entire night wondering why Malik abandoned me and didn't wait for me to return.

The next day, I awoke late because I was too tired, hurriedly changed, and intended to return to Sir's residence.

I heard Shaadi shouting to me as I stood outside waiting for the driver. She wanted to remind me about my flights, saying that all of my classmates had completed their domestic flights and were about to begin their international flights.

I assured her that she had nothing to worry about. I'm keeping track of the time and will return to duty soon. "Let's see," she smiled and replied.

Until I arrived at Sir Malik's residence, I had a thousand thoughts. I had a key this time, and when I entered the garden, I noticed roughly twenty large boxes labeled with my name. Why should my delivery go to Malik's house, I was confused. Second, I'd never gone shopping before, so what could they be and why were there so many?

I opened one and found bedsheets, blankets, and pillows. When I opened the other one, it was full of crystal cups, plates, and other culinary items.

I started checking for the sender address and discovered that everything had been sent by Shaadi!

I don't know how I'm going to explain all of this to Malik. "I never got to know the actuality of your presence at my place," he said as he walked out of the house.

Last night, you invited me to your property for the most expensive party of the year, and your sweetheart turned out to be a Prince who discreetly bought you a diamond necklace…and now this!

"What was your aunt's thought process? She assumed I wouldn't have anything in my house for her sweet niece to sleep on, or that I wouldn't have appropriate plates to serve you food? Look at the size of the TV, she wanted you to eat in crystal!

"How many times have I asked if you want TV and offered to bring it from upstairs to your room!"

Natural came to a halt and exclaimed, "I'm so hungry, I can't go any more until I eat something," and we both proceeded to the kitchen. She inquired about my favorite university subject. I told her I wanted to be a nurse. She smiled and said I have a lovely face and a compassionate heart, which she said would be ideal for my future career.

Sir Malik didn't want to bother us, so Natural served and took his meal. We sat and ate lunch together. She asked if I had ever been in love, but I didn't know what to say because I rarely leave the house, so how could I meet someone? I'm always researching or writing something! I replied to her.

# Chapter 8
# The Time After

Natural asked if we could go on a walk and I said yes. I didn't mind because I was interested in seeing how their neighborhoods looked. We both went after she left a note for Sir Malik.

A lovely park was only a short distance away. We went for a walk on a treadmill. It was beautiful weather, so we did some stretching together and found an empty bench to sit on after a bit.

She stated, "I didn't know how to mend everything that day, Malik was so pissed at me that I handed him complete control."

He merely requested that I leave his premises. I was heartbroken, but I was determined not to give up. This was exactly what Shaadi and others had predicted, but I stuck up for myself and asked for another chance.

This will never happen again, I promised him, and this is merely a misunderstanding; my aunt will never do such a thing! I need to call and make arrangements to pick them up and return them all.

I informed him about Prince Albert, and Shaadi tried her hardest to get us together, but she was unsuccessful. I informed him about the island and the lake.

I also reminded him that, because of the way I was raised, it is simpler for me to be buddies with males than with girls, and urged that he must believe Albert is a friend to me, which he knows very well. "He is terribly lonely," I said simply, looking into his eyes. "Only a true friend can sense that!"

Next, I dialed Shaadi's number, and she appeared to be waiting for my call just near the phone!

I didn't want to respond to what she did because I knew she was a strong woman in the country and it would be easy for her to harm Malik or seek vengeance, so I simply thanked her for her concern and assured her that I was in excellent hands and that Sir Malik had supplied me with everything I needed. Malik was hearing on our discussions.

Shaadi stated that she only wanted me to understand who I was and where I came from, but that if I didn't require any of the objects, she would arrange for their pickup.

I thanked her again for her patience, gently requested that she let me know ahead of time if she made any decisions, and we both said our goodbyes and hung up the phone.

In the garden, I left everything as it was. Shaadi dispatched her boys two days later to return all of the boxes and clean up the garden. To be honest, I was completely confused and unsure of where to begin again. I could never see Malik because he was constantly out.

Malik was aware that it was New Year's Eve, so why was he punishing me in this manner? I created one of our traditional dinners, as well as other side dishes, with the help of a cooking book. I dressed myself and sat in front of the television, anticipating his arrival later that evening!

I imagined us sitting together after midnight, with him kissing me and me telling him how much I love him, but I wasn't so lucky! I heard one of the windows cracks as I was waiting for him. I assumed that one of the old tree's huge limbs had fallen and smashed the glass as a result of the intense wind.

I ran to see which window it was, but all of the sofas were taken with various students who had come to join the art class, virtually all of whom had their equipment with them, some of whom had notebooks in their hands, while others had paint brushes and things for their paintings!

I slapped my face awake, but I could still see them, and they could see me. Some of them also brought their musical instruments with them, such as violins and guitars.

They were all greeting me, and several even tried to shake my hand! Among them all, I noticed the same female, who was regularly there to cause me problems! What did she want to do to me this time, I wondered? Why is it that she is always on the lookout for me?

She drew closer and took my hand in hers. I could feel the heat from her palm, and she handed me a small piece of paper. I explained that I was in the hospital because of the glasses she broke the last time. I told her to leave me alone and to quit bothering me.

I looked around while talking to her and saw no other people; it was just the two of us. She appeared to be terrified, pointing to the antique room, and suddenly vanished into the darkness! The hall was suddenly restored to its previous state.

I read the paper. "Help Me," it said in red letters.

I was going insane, and I was fed up with keeping it to myself all the time. I was alone and it was beyond midnight.

That night, I wished my mother was still alive and I cried like a small girl who wanted love and care. What was going on with me was out of the ordinary.

I was daydreaming and conversing with the wall, and I could hear voices. With this health concern, how could I return to work?

However, I don't recall falling asleep, and when I awoke the next morning, I was in my pajamas!

I wanted to go to church on the first day of the year, I dressed up and exited my room to find Malik preparing breakfast on the hall table, which included fresh bread, cream cheese, bacon, an omelet, coffee, pancakes, and cranberry juice! I was so taken aback that I forgot to say morning!

He approached me and wished me a happy new year, then invited me to breakfast. He stated that he would drop me off at Church later.

I quickly sat at the table, thinking no one would want to miss that breakfast.

He asked me what I liked to do after church while I was still speechless.

When I asked him how I got into my pajamas last night, he just stared at me and said, "How should I know?"

(What a stupid question, I realized.)

"My purse was taken yesterday, along with my driver's license, insurance cards, and money!" he continued. "I requested Jamal's assistance.

"We went to the police station together, and because it was so packed and half of their personnel was on vacation, they let us wait till midnight. It was already New Year's Eve when I finished and returned home!"

"I wanted to call and apologize for being late, but Jamal assured me that we would be finished shortly!"

I had no right to be angry with him because he was late for a valid reason; it was not his fault! Jamal, on the other hand, had irritated me by refusing to allow him contact and notify me!

I was debating whether or not to reveal any details from last night before I started speaking.

"New Year's Eves have not been joyful for me at anyway, since my parents died on that fateful night," I said. "I hoped being away from home would allow me to forget about that dreadful night, but I suppose I can't."

After hearing me, Sir Malik was quite disappointed! He sat down next to me, took my hand in his, and said, "I'm not sure if taking your hand in mine will allow me to cross the red line or not, but I am very sorry, I can perfectly understand your feelings for your parents, because I didn't have any of mine by my side too."

My tale is very different from yours. I wanted they had drowned as well, so I could easily declare, "I miss them!" They did, however, leave a lot of wounds on my soul.

My father was a musician who played a variety of musical instruments.

He used to perform a wide range of concerts on a regular basis.

He had his private tutoring in the residence the most of the time.

"My mother was a singer, she used to sing in nightclubs," he added while still holding my hand.

Then my father will notice her brilliance and provide her with a larger opportunity, and she will finally become renowned. She sang on TV shows, her voice was broadcast on the radio, and she later began recording her own cassettes.

This is how they met and fell in love with one other. I was born after a year of their marriage, which was probably horrible time for my parents. They were both unprepared! My grandmother or a caregiver would always leave me alone! I'm not sure if we ever had a party or a celebration together.

Dad had performances to attend, and Mum was always working in the studio! My father initially complained about my mother's absence, but I eventually discovered that he was only acting.

He had a covert relationship with his students who came to our house for private sessions; regrettably, he wasn't only taking advantage of young females; he was also exploiting young boys!

I'll never forget the last time I saw him in the kitchen with his student!

My mother, on the other hand, was involved with her producer and was unconcerned about what was going on.

She was content as long as my father did not infringe on her freedom.

Their relationship lasted until I was twelve years old, at which point I broke up with them. My mum intended to flee with her boyfriend to another country.

I recall her holding my hand on the day she departed, telling me that as a mother, she did everything she could to raise me. I'm on my own for the time being! She then walked away!

Dad had HIV and died in the hospital a year after my mother had gone. I was on my own.

Only GOD knows what I went through till I reassembled all of my shattered pieces! I was alone in this place for many days and nights, without money or food!

We chuckled and left the park when Natural jumped up and said, "Let's go back before Malik gets hungry again." We were both quiet on the walk back; I'm guessing we were both thinking about the same thing!

Then she started working quickly, while I was roaming around the garden looking for a suitable tree for my sketching! I could tell she was rushing to finish her work so she could join me.

# Chapter 9
# Fallen Behind

Sir Malik wanted to give me a ride since it was becoming dark, but Natural insisted on having dinner first and then going! I said that I needed to stay with my father, and that he wouldn't eat without me!

So, I left their house with Sir, and on the way, I was a little hesitant to bring up any topic with him, but he dropped the first inquiry, asking how I felt about Natural.

I told him she's unique, someone who appears tough on the outside but is gentle and sensitive on the inside! Also, breathtakingly attractive!

"She was incredibly different and difficult to discover," he continued, "and it took me a long time to figure out why she was at my house all that time." Imagine a gorgeous, young, and extremely clever lady knocking on your door and requesting to be hired as your servant! Later on, you'll learn she's the first Pilot lady, descended from one of the country's wealthiest families!

"She was like a puzzle piece, and no matter how hard I tried to be close to her, I would have discovered even more astounding facts about her. After the first week of her stay, I began to develop feelings for her! But we were too dissimilar;

my mind held me back while my emotions pushed me onward."

He pulled over to the side of the road, lowered the shutters, and asked if I had any free time. "Please don't worry about me; I'm only here to write your story; please go on!" I begged him.

He thanked me and went on to say: Have you heard about my folks from Natural? Yes, I said, and he continued, "Growing up in this kind of home forced me to make the decision to control my inner desires as a man, or, to put it another way, my physical needs!

"I went to a lot of places seeking for individuals who could help me, and a lot of them offered me surgery, but that wasn't what I wanted; I wanted to have it but not use it!"

I didn't want to get physically engaged with any lady after what I'd seen about my folks!

Because of their actions, I felt compelled to punish myself. I recall being terrified. There was a cupboard in my room that I used to hide in whenever my dad had a lesson at our house.

My Grandma raised me; she was not allowed in our home, and my mother would occasionally drop me off at her house and neglect to pick me up!

I came to Nepal and stayed for several months to work on being the person I wanted to be. My feelings began to return after meeting Natural. I was at odds with myself; on one hand, I desperately wanted to be with her, but on the other, I didn't want to abandon my beliefs.

I vividly recall how frightened I was the day she damaged her feet. I was constantly praying for her health and begging God to help me pass this exam.

I couldn't imagine being with her because she was a member of the royal family and I was just a regular person! However, I can't possibly imagine a day without her!

I was astounded to learn how wealthy she was on Christmas Eve! That night, her aunt told me to start a fight and ask Natural to leave as soon as possible.

She even revealed to me that she is soon to be engaged to Prince, who will divorce his wife and marry Natural.

She informed me that Natural is too immature, that she has only allowed her to gain experience for a short period of time, and that it is best if I assist her in returning to reality and beginning her life and bright future!

"I'm not sure why I followed Natural that night, but I did." I felt utterly brokenhearted after hearing her balcony talk with Albert. I despised myself for finally taking the route I had been avoiding for so long! Jamal was the one who got me involved in the whole incident, and I got into a fight with him that night.

I was frightened of losing her, but it was also too much for me to manage all at once.

Shaadi also intended to push me down by sending these pricey households, but I received her message and was forced to stand in front of her; this was not how I used to deal with people, so I decided to give Natural or myself a second chance to be by her side and help her finish what she came for!

People at work were asking me about her, and some even stopped me on the way home and told if I could set up an interview with Natural!

Her aunt was the country's wealthiest entrepreneur, and she was Prince Albert's sweetheart and pilot! I was too afraid of being rejected to speak up and tell her the truth about my feelings since I had all of these thoughts in my head.

I could see she cared about me, but I had no idea she was in love with me. I assumed that after she moved in, she felt terrible for my loneliness and wanted to help me because she knew I wouldn't get along with anyone else!

He took a breath and then started the car, saying, I'll let Natural tell the rest of the story; all I wanted to do was give a hint about my side of the story. "I arrived at the hotel after ten o'clock, and my father was still waiting for me in the lobby. Sir, I expressed my gratitude for the ride. At the restaurant's dinner table, I told my father the entire story."

He was excited and pity for both of them that they couldn't just have a regular talk without thinking about a hundred topics! After breakfast the next day, I decided to travel to Sir Malik's residence on my own and leave my father to rest.

It was lunchtime when I arrived at Sir's place, and Natural was the one who opened the gate and inquired if I was all right.

I apologized and explained that I needed some time to clear my head and figure out the best method to write the story! She invited me upstairs because she wanted to show me her gold medals and awards from when she was my age.

Then she showed me Sir's office and their bedroom, saying that Sir Malik doesn't like people up there, but he had made an exception for me.

Between the two bedrooms upstairs was a little hallway with two seats and a small table. So we sat there, she had already prepared tea sets and biscuits, and after a little discussion on the house's history and room styles, she resumed her story:

I had a lot to say to him that day, but after hearing his story, I didn't want to bother him about my mental health or family problems, so I kept my thoughts to myself for a long.

He drove me to the church after breakfast and waited in the taxi.

He gave me his recently published book on that day.

I was overjoyed. He stated that I am the first to possess it.

He asked if I had read any of his novels, to which I replied that I had read them all, some of them three or four times because the first time wasn't enough for me to grasp the plot, so I would keep reading until I was immersed in it!

He was taken aback when he heard those remarks.

I sincerely thanked him.

I was on a break at that day, so I decided to read his book. I attempted to contact Shaadi to express my best wishes, but she was unavailable.

Malik left a letter saying he would purchase pizza for dinner while he was gone. I began reading the book while lying in my bed, pausing to get a cup of tea in the meantime. When I returned to the room, the book was missing; I assumed I had left it in the corridor, but there was no sign of it!

I noticed my suitcase on the bed and went over to open it. I saw that there were a lot of baby garments packed, and I discovered Sir's book underneath them all. I knew it had something to do with her since she was around and I could sense her presence. I didn't have time to be terrified when I peeked out the window and saw her standing next to the pool.

When I saw the front gate light turn on, I knew Malik was around; she simply leapt into the pool and vanished. I expected her to do that, so I went back inside the suitcase to check for the clothing, but they were still there! I hurriedly packed them and tucked them beneath the bed.

I didn't want Malik to know about my bizarre day and night fantasies, since it was too early!

Only one thing struck me: these dreams weren't just about the Sir home; they were also about me, and I was carrying them around with me!

I attempted to convey that everything was well. I asked whether we had a visitor because he had three boxes of pizza in his hand. "Yes, Jamal wanted to come and wish you well, so I invited him to supper."

I dashed to the kitchen and began preparing some drinks, but my gaze was fixed on the pool.

I assumed she was still around, waiting for Sir to leave so she could annoy me, but what could I do to stop having nightmares?

I needed to be treated before flying; otherwise, I would endanger the lives of hundreds of others. What if she enters the captain's cabin as well? I'll have to talk to her, then they will denounce me as a delusional pilot!

I heard the bell ring, and Jamal was there as well; I figured I could open up to him and beg for assistance, but I wasn't sure he wouldn't tell Shaadi! After all, they were long-time friends and business partners.

I carried the tea set into the hall and greeted him; he wished me a happy new year, and they both sat at the table, inviting me to join them.

Jamal said: Your aunt was expecting you at the royal church today; I told him that there is no such thing as a royal or ordinary church; it is a place for everyone; I chose to go to a different church today; the prayers are the same regardless of which one you choose!

Both of them agreed by shaking their heads. I was expecting Jamal to begin relaying Shaddi's messages, so I inquired, "Has she asked you to be here tonight?"

"I gave up, your aunt had obliged me to encourage you to come back by next week!" he replied, raising his hands. Before going live, she wants you to rehearse. She's concerned about you, to be honest! "You don't look very healthy and have lost weight, which is why I've come to find out why."

"Has my friend pushed you around and given you too much work to do?" He inquired.

"Sir Malik is a respectable gentleman, as anticipated," I replied. He has never asked for anything, he performs the majority of the housework, and he gives me lots of breaks. I began to diet since I felt I was overweight!

Malik was staring at me and smiling sweetly. Finally, I was afraid that if Jamal kept asking me questions, I would open up about my nightmares, and whatever I had built up to that point would be rejected.

I considered excused myself for a bathroom break.

I sat on the ground and locked myself in. I figured, raising boys, sleeping in a coffin, and becoming a pilot were all things I'd done before, and I wouldn't let one dumb dream hold me back. I'm not going to give up now that I've gotten so close to Malik! That Nightmare should be over at this point.

We all slept late that night, and they questioned me about my trips, after which they both began relating their stories of their first flights. Jamal requested that Malik read us some of his most recent poems.

He said yes. He was talking about a woman's appearance inside those lines, which made me envious. I wished he'd used all those phrases to describe me instead!

The next day, Sir left the house early, and I began cleaning. The entrance to the antique room had been opened, so I decided to walk inside and have a closer look...

Malik told me to leave this room alone and not to touch anything because it was priceless! There were plenty of books, carpets, mugs, Jars, night lamps, paintings, and much more, but there was one thing that stood out: varied colored scarves, pants, and skirts!

On them, I could still smell the scent!

When the phone started ringing, I bolted from the room. The door slammed shut behind me, scaring me to death! I responded, it was Shaadi, and hearing the voice of a living human was the nicest thing that could have happened to me at the time!

Albert is coming to see her tomorrow, she said. I can join them if I want. They intend to visit the family farm! I promised I'd let her know by the evening. I despised myself because I had never learned to say No!

Natural seemed irritated by this part of the story, so she stomped up and motioned for me to follow her into the garden. I noticed a football game in the corner and asked her if she wanted to join in. She was ecstatic and asked if I knew how to play; I said that I didn't, but I knew how it worked!

I attempted to compete with her, but she proved to be too difficult to deal with! I informed her that Malik can't play with her because she's too fast! While trying to score, she started laughing and remarked, "His migraine always starts, and he takes off!" I couldn't stop laughing.

She then showed me how to relax and went into the kitchen to bring me lemonade that she had made earlier.

I told her it was fine if she needed to do some of her work, and that I could finish my drawing in the Garden. She accepted my offer and said she simply needed to marinate the steak for supper. She didn't waste any time, and came back in no time, saying that the portion she's about to talk about is the one that Malik despised, so she'd best get started before he arrives!

"That day, I really wanted to get out of the house since something was bugging me at that spot. I didn't have the guts to continue and question Malik about anything I observed in the antique room! I knew if he found out about me slipping into that room, he'd be furious."

I didn't want to start a quarrel again, but leaving Sir Malik and going to meet Albert was also not the appropriate thing to do; he wanted to be with me as his partner, not as a friend; understanding this part for Albert was difficult! I considered asking Sir for permission for a day, and if he approved, I would inform Shaadi!

I contemplated finding a specialist who could assist me; I didn't know anyone who was a therapist, but Shaadi was sure he knew a few. I was terrified of being discovered and worried about my future.

My mother was suffering from some sort of mental ailment at the time, Shaadi told me, and she was taking medicines to help her feel better. I never inquired as to the nature of her illness or the identity of her physician! I was hoping to find a solution to my troubles by following her profile. Before going, I needed to finish Malik's book.

To get into the hall, I couldn't open the door. I knew the cursed girl was there, so I yelled, "Enough with your games; I'm not afraid of you; let me be and leave this place!"

When the door opened, I was undecided about going in or staying out. I was terrified at the time, but I didn't want to give up! When I was younger, our boys' group used to make up ghost stories. They will harass us much more if they sense our dread! I couldn't tell if it was a ghost or if it was all in my brain! Only I could see and feel whatever it was!

After battling, I decided to go inside, the door closed behind me, I remained calm, and walked to my room to retrieve the book, which was once again gone. I saw my suitcase was out on the bed, so I opened it and discovered that the infant clothing was still inside, as well as the book!

I requested Natural to stop telling her story since I was getting goose bumps on my arms and the story was starting to scare me! She stared at me, frightened, and went to fetch a glass of cool water. I assured her that I needed only a few moments' rest. Soon after, I urged her to continue, but she hesitated, so I persisted, telling her that I had to hear the rest of the story no matter what!

She took my hand in hers and stated that the day they both decided to ask me to come write their story, she wasn't sure I could take it, but Sir Malik was adamant that I could.

I told her, "I'm not used to hearing these types of things, and I'm a little terrified," but something inside me compelled me to continue, "so please tell me precisely what occurred, no matter how I feel!" She then turned to face me and said, smiling. "I'm certain he made the right decision now."

Do you recall me telling you about the piece of paper she gave me on New Year's Eve with the words HELP written on it? The same material was used to separate the book's pages. I simply informed her that I couldn't help her because no one believes me! How can I tell anyone about her? People would think I'm insane, and no one will accept!

Everything fell silent quickly, including the clock, I sat on the floor and began praying by closing eyes. I don't recall ever praying like way before that day on my own. That day, though, was different. After finishing prayer, I felt sleepy and couldn't move my legs, so I hauled myself up to the bed and fell asleep as soon as my head on the pillow.

I heard my name numerous times, saw Malik standing next to the bed with a glass of water, I inquired what time it was. Then he sat next to me and said, "It's dark."

I told him there was food in the kitchen and that he could have it if he wanted it, but he urged me to forget about eating since I had a fever.

To get my temperature down, he gave me a cup of water and two pills. To be honest, I tried to get up, but I couldn't keep my balance because I was so exhausted.

He inquired me what had occurred? Why haven't I eaten anything and have been waiting so long?

I told him everything I had done that day, but I didn't mention about my bizarre visions! Then he remarked that I'd been really weak and that he needed to take better care of me! I came here to assist Malik, and now he is the one who is constantly looking after me!

The phone rang, and Malik went to answer it; it was Shaadi, and she spoke with Sir Malik; he then put the phone down and walked up to me, asking how I was going to join my family tomorrow in this condition.

I say, "first and foremost, I have not confirmed. Second, I'm just tired, possibly anxious, and I'll be back on track the next day!"

Shaadi had requested him to inform me that she was sending a car to fetch me!

What a calamity! I didn't know what to do, and I didn't have many alternatives at the moment, so I decided to wait till morning. Malik chose to sleep on the couch in order to keep an eye on me! I ate a bland soup and went back to bed, but I couldn't relax since I was worried about the next day and my situation!

I could see her the entire night because she was sitting next to Malik on the sofa! She simply wants me to know that she is always there!

The light in my room was turned on, and I went back down on my bed and began praying once again; I had no idea what was going on, and I needed assistance and support! Only God was aware of what was taking place!

At midnight, I noticed Malik waking up and coming into the room to check on me a few times; each time he was in the room, I pretended to be asleep so he could be confident I was fine and go back to sleep!

When I awoke at 6 a.m., my legs were alright, if a little weak, but I was able to go to the bathroom and walk around the home. I was overjoyed, and Malik was awake as well, warning me not to get too excited and injure myself again, which he was right about!

# Chapter 10
# Confusion Is Nothing New

Natural was one of my favorite characters, she couldn't stay still for long periods of time; she would extend her arms and legs while sitting, or even spin her ankles.

It reminds her that she is still living, she used to say.

That day, Malik was very interested in learning what I wanted to do, so I told him it was best for me to take a short break. When he heard out, he had no emotion, which made me even more irritated.

He handed me an envelope and said, "This is your pay; it's not much, but it's what we bargained on!" He finally said, "He doesn't mind if I don't come back at all if I'm done collecting the experience that I was seeking for."

I became furious and questioned him if he was tired of seeing me.

He stated that he no longer wants me as a servant and that it is now time for me to consider my options. My trips begin in a week, and I am in no way physically fit. He respectfully requested that I quit doing whatever it was that I had come for and return to my normal routine!

Those words he was telling me would not bother me if I was still thinking like a boy! All of them made logic, but as a girl, I was devastated, or more accurately, disappointed, since after all these days, I couldn't get him to love me!

I could feel my body heating up, so I took my time and said, "I will do that as soon as I locate a good housemaid for you." I'd like to teach her and make sure she can handle everything around the house!

"As I said, I am no longer in need of a servant or maybe I will sell this enormous house and obtain an apartment so I will not need help any longer," Sir Malik remarked, smiling. I was shocked when I completed packing that day.

I didn't want to say farewell, I held him, and I guess he was having a great time since he was holding me so tight. What a moment, I wanted to give him the magic word and tell him I'm dying for his love, but I didn't. I realized there was a part of me left in that house as the automobile drove, and I turned around to see he was still waiting outside!

I requested the driver to pull over to the side after we were out of his sight, and I got down, shouted, and sat on the ground crying! It's a good thing there weren't many other people on the road! You should've seen the driver's face as he leapt out of the car and dashed up to me!

On the way back to the car, he assisted me, and I realized Shaadi had to do something about the situation! Later, I learned that what she had whispered to Malik's ear at the Christmas party had something to do with that day's disaster.

I was trying to glue my broken pieces back together and didn't want to tell anyone, so the driver promised not to say anything!

Everything seemed usual at my aunt's, the servants were preparing for the Prince's arrival, and I ran into Shaadi at the front gate, who hugged me and inquired why I was limping! I informed her that I had sustained an injury while playing football!

She said, with a sad expression on her face, "When will I quit behaving like a jerk and start acting like a lady? I still have no idea how to dress properly, style my hair, walk like a lady, or even apply cosmetics! What makes you think someone could admire you?"

I didn't waste any time and walked straight to my room, where I stood in front of the mirror, staring at myself! She was correct; my feelings may have shifted on the inside, but the way I appeared on the outside was dreadful! I hadn't even brushed my hair, and I only had four sets of clothes with me in front of Malik, which I was constantly wearing. I never tried to grab his attention!

I was never taught how to be a woman by anyone.

Furthermore, no of how I looked, if Malik found out about my mental illness, he would have left me! I was attempting to persuade myself of my failure in some way.

I went to take a warm bath and discovered a set of garments, including a skirt, gowns, blouses, and other items, along with a message that read, "You have lost the first one, don't lose up on the second." Shaadi's' handwriting was actually on the page.

I chose one dress and intended to return to bed. One of the assistants approached me and instructed me to prepare for Prince Albert's arrival. To let my hair dry, I combed it and left it open! Then I went down and joined the queue of helpers to greet the prince!

Shaadi went ahead and greeted him; she motioned for me to do the same, but I didn't bother! He was the one who approached me and extended his hand to shake mine.

He accompanied me to the Hall.

I invited him to join me in the lobby, and Albert consented, so we both walked there. Shaadi afforded us some privacy by asking his men to leave us alone.

I offered him tea and inquired about his purpose for being here. He brought various explanations, but they all ended up with me!

I was so impatient that I wanted him to change his mind and return!

Before telling him anything, I attempted to calm down and practice my words; after all, he was a Prince! I need to be more careful with what I say! I began questioning him about where I had been and what I had been doing all this time!

He claimed that he had known everything from the beginning, but that he wanted me to go find what I was seeking for and then return to him!

"It's not simple to live with someone you love; try to keep your emotions hidden! I first sensed him amongst his books, and then when I arrived at his home, I sensed his pure heart! I went there to experience LOVE, and I did, in some ways, but I also got the chance to stay and be with someone who could one day be my Prince!" I stated.

"My body is entirely yours if you want it, but my heart belongs to him. I choose to live with Malik, not this, because I simply want to be myself, not someone who must wear a mask to satisfy everyone! I can't accomplish anything on my own in this house; everything is dictated to me; even my clothing are chosen by someone else!"

We can't be lovers, I told Albert! However, I am willing to be his mate. I told him that we should simply be buddies because right now in my life, I need someone to talk to and who understands me more than a partner or a sweetheart.

I was the one who was speaking the whole time, and I didn't even let him have his tea; perhaps I was too unhappy and wanted to find a way to unload my hatred on him, and he was right around the corner!

Albert was completely deafeningly silent throughout the entire process. I'm sure he's never been greeted so warmly!

He got up and asked if I would let him leave; I turned away and replied yes! To be honest, I have no recollection of what happened after that; one of the assistants said I lost my balance and spilled the entire tea set from the table, and that I was asleep for a half day! I suspect I've been poisoned!

Shaadi was seated by my bed, holding my hand, when I opened my eyes! I inquired as to what had occurred. She informed me that I had lost my equilibrium and had only recently awoken.

She also claimed that she had phoned Sir Malik and reprimanded him for sending me out of his house in this state. She expressed her dissatisfaction by saying, "I went to his place in wonderful health and returned unwell."

Shaadi pretended to be frustrated with Malik, and she would have taught him a lesson if it was not because of Jamal. She also says that despite my illness, he knew I couldn't perform or serve and had asked me to go! Man, you're a jerk!

I told her it was entirely my decision; he never invites me to join him, so please let him be! I also informed her that she desired my presence, and he complied with her wishes and released me. I'm completely hers now. From now on, I'll dance to every song she plays, and yeah, she succeeded once again.

"Doctor asked you to come for some critical examinations tomorrow at our family hospital," Shaadi stated as he rose up. She'll be there as well. Then requested somebody to serve my food in my room, and walked out of the room with a sad face.

Why was I doing all of this, I wondered, and why was I being so cruel to Shaadi? She was the last person I had left!

Even though I didn't give him a chance to speak, I realized I had been rude to him.

I made the decision to act more maturely, keeping my troubles to myself.

I had completely forgotten who or how I had been poisoned, so I went to the dressing table, looked for the brush, and discovered a note on the bed!

"I can't leave without saying goodbye," Albert said, "so tell me whenever you are ready." I was relieved to know he was still there. When I emerged from my room, I noticed that one of the helpers was watching my room as Shaadi had instructed.

I knew where Albert's room was, so I walked straight to him, knowing he was expecting me!

"Before you continue fighting with me, I have something unique for you, it is really valuable, and that was the actual reason I came here to deliver it to you myself," he said.

There was a notepad there, and when I opened it, it pointed to the Islands, where I could discover pink dolphins.

He claimed that after that day, he began researching their environments. All of his hard work had paid off in the form of notebooks!

I was embarrassed, and I told him today that Sir Malik wanted me to go... I was heartbroken and in excruciating pain. He simply showed up at the worst possible time! Otherwise, I have always appreciated and will continue to honor our friendship.

Albert said he understands what I'm going through because he's in the same situation!

I'm worried about Malik's love because I'm not receiving any responses, and he's desperate for attention and love from me but isn't getting any, so we're in the same boat. He expressed himself.

He stated he understands why I was willing to go to any length to be with Him. Even though you know you're going to be rejected, there's a deep feeling that you just want to be there!

We were both the same, he was right!

He stated that he would leave the next day when I received the results from my physician.

Malik is a smart guy, Albert informed me, but he didn't want to risk it because of your lifestyles and family! It's not simple, believe me!

"I have a wife, and believe me, it is tough to keep her content, because her expectations are too high, and it is not her mistake; she has been offered whatever she wants from the start, and it makes it too tough for anyone to live with her, because her perspective on life is different!" He stated his case.

"Malik knew your affection and your care," he said. "I am a guy, and trust me when I say that! He made the best decision he could at the moment. At the very least, I'd be able to get you back!" We both burst out laughing.

I was relieved that Albert was so mature and unconcerned about anything I had told him upon his arrival. Finally, I was relieved that he could be my friend!

It was eight o'clock in the evening when I checked my watch. Natural was also oblivious to how long she had been chatting. She informed me that we had entirely forgotten about lunch and dinner! "I took care of that part," Sir Malik shouted.

He moved closer and proceeded, sensing that we were at a particularly delicate point in the story, he didn't want to bother us and wanted to wait till Natural decided to pause and reflect on her sad spouse for a moment!

Natural approached him, kissed him on the cheek, and exclaimed, "I constantly think of you!"

Sir Malik was handed some refreshments in a container and told me that my father had called and said he would pick me up. He's been in the garden for an hour now, waiting for me! He didn't want him to call me since the story was too important to him!

I was overjoyed, and I rushed to the Garden to see my father, where we both expressed our gratitude for their thoughtfulness and returned to our hotel with a cap.

# Chapter 11
# Sharpest Words

I had breakfast and proceeded straight to their home, as is customary. Now that I was an expert and also understood the shortcuts, I was the one advising the taxi driver on which route to take to save time!

I requested that my father not be concerned about me. I know how to get back, and I need to give Natural more opportunity to finish her story; each time he arrives, she must pause her story because of me! He happily agreed.

On the way, I stopped at a flower shop and bought a bouquet of flowers for Natural. It was a day dedicated to women.

She was expecting me and was overjoyed to see me with flowers.

She expressed gratitude to me. Sir was also present, and he claimed that I had made his work more difficult this time because the simplest option for him on Women's Day was to buy a flower for Natural!

We were all giggling!

Sir insisted that I accompany him to his gallery to view some of his works! This, I informed him, was the nicest present I could have received on this particular day. The

Gallery was placed underground, the lighting was great, and he showed me one of his very first paintings, which sold the most.

There were lots more, and he patiently described a several to me!

Natural was waiting for us in the Garden, where she prepared a delightful chamomile tea that was quite pleasant. Sir had planned to go before that, but he claimed that his parts will arrive shortly, and he would be able to speak for me as well!

Admittedly, it's always nicer when she speaks! he added.

Natural sat and reread the narrative to herself till she reached the point where she stopped yesterday and said: "The next day, I got up early to go to the hospital." Albert was not supposed to be seen in public for two reasons: first, his wife, and second, paparazzi! As a result, he stayed.

Getting to the hospital that day was a disaster. An explosion occurred in one of the cement factories, and all of the unlucky workers who were injured were sent to various hospitals.

I wished I could assist them that it was so heartbreaking to see.

We made it to the radiography and laboratories. To complete all of the tests, it took me almost two hours. Shaadi was treated so well by the doctor that he instructed us to leave and that he would contact us soon the results were received.

Albert began inquiring about everything as soon as I arrived at the house, and he appeared to be really worried. After Shaadi notified Sir Malik about me, I was hoping he might call or When I inquired about Jamal from Shaadi, she informed me that he had gone on a business trip and would return in two weeks. Shaadi looked to be trying to limit them; I was sick, but not foolish! She was overjoyed that Albert and I were becoming closer. I knew she'd been looking forward to this moment for quite some time.

I recall asking Albert if his wife was aware of his visits to our home. She is the one who is encouraging me to come to you, he explained. Her spy has reported everything because she knows you're in love with Malik and have no interest in me.

"Since she was a child, she has been involved with the son of her private instructor. Because of their family's social position, they were not permitted to marry. So, the arranged marriage took place, and she ended up marrying the wrong man, which happened to be me!

"We decided to be open and honest with one other about our relationships while keeping them hidden from the rest of the world! She is obviously with him at the times I am here! She refuses to accept I've never had an emotional bond with you! She's asked me to use various gifts to persuade you, but I've informed her you're not an ordinary girl."

"I was taken aback and had a million questions about their decision to approach him! But the most important question was what would happen if she became pregnant."

Albert responded, "Easy, get rid of the youngster or I'll get rid of three of them at the same time!"

I inquired of him: "Why did he consent to such ridiculous ideas? Why did you marry in the first place? Could have waited longer till he finds true love?"

"These are fairy tales," he continued, "and as we both know, they don't exist!"

The doctor contacted the next day to ask if he might come to our house and personally deliver all of the results. Something wasn't quite right with me at the moment!

When the doctor arrived in the afternoon, Shaadi led him into her conference room, where he sat us all, including Albert, and began questioning me about my previous health.

Then he said, "There is something that has been seen in my scan, and it is sadly termed a Brain Tumor!"

I just grinned and thought to myself, "My head and heart seem to be broken."

Finally, he began to describe what a brain tumor is, how many stages there are to the illness, and how to treat it. Shaadi kept her face covered the entire time so no one could see her cry! But there were no tears to be found.

To be honest, I didn't have anything to risk at the moment, so I didn't mind. The doctor expected me to react in some way to the circumstance, and Albert was monitoring me out so that if I sobbed, he could hurry and console me!

I politely inquired about the case, and the doctor was delighted to provide additional information.

"You can't really stop a brain tumor," he stated. "Avoiding environmental dangers like smoking and high exposure to radiation can help you prevent having a brain tumor."

"The larger the proportion, the more dangerous the tumor: class 1 and 2 brain tumors are benign (non-cancerous) tumors that grow slowly.

So, mine was at the start of stage two, where the tumor grows slowly but has the potential to spread to surrounding tissues.

Second level tumors are more likely to relapse following surgery, and some can progress to cancer.

"The tumor may finally destroy you, depending on your age at diagnosis. Alternatively, you could have a full life and die of something else. It will be determined by the type of tumor, its location in the brain, and how it reacts to treatment.

"Even if your brain tumor cannot be cured, treatment may decrease it and slow its progression.

"Surgery, radiation, or chemotherapy may be required. Alternatively, a combination of these treatments may be used."

Oh, the doctor was ready for any of my queries, and I was extremely pleased with his answers! still one thing he neglected to mention was the symptoms, which I soon inquired about, and to which he kindly replied:

The symptoms can be:

"Headaches that can be severe and go worse with activity or early in the morning.

"Seizures. Changes in personality or memory. Vomiting or nausea. He also mentioned drowsiness, sleep, and memory issues."

He asked me to take my time and think about it, then come to him when I was ready so he could begin the treatment.

Natural smiled at me and remarked, "Can you believe I already know everything the doctor told me that day?" I felt like one of those kids who had to memorize every single word in order to graduate from medical school.

She went on to say:

Albert and Shaadi had a long day ahead of them, and they were both wondering about me or how my mundane life would end. Shaadi expressed her dissatisfaction.

After the doctor had departed, I approached her, took her hand in mine, and said, "Shaadi, the way you're acting, it's as if tomorrow is my funeral! This could happen to anyone, but God chose me, and I'm okay with it. Instead of sitting in sorrow for me, you should be cheering me on!"

"She's right," Albert remarked, laughing, "I believe the one with the tumor is us, not her!"

Shaadi realized she was overreacting and abruptly halted it! I informed them that if they would allow it, I needed some time alone. Before I confirm any treatment with a doctor, I need to consider again.

Albert helped me leave the room because he wanted me to accompany him to the garden. I emerged from the conference room to find a cane and one of the aides standing in front of the gate.

I was fine, but Shaadi and Albert were doing their best to prepare me for what was about to happen. It did not appeal to me. Shaadi was itching to get some slumber! Everything was meticulously planned and executed one after the other.

Near the waterfall, there was a lovely bench, and I remembered hiding behind it anytime I needed to get away from Shaadi! We sat down. He was concerned about me, and I was anxious about Malik, whom I missed.

I gave him an honest look and urged him not to treat to me like a toddler; I assume I was old enough to understand my situation. I told him.

Natural came to a halt and stated, "There's something I'd like to tell you here," before continuing, I requested my aunt to send me to the camp one summer. All the females were waiting for a handsome boy who used to brag about being a boxer to notice them!

His friend used to organize a fight between him and another poor person every Friday, out of the teacher's sight, and girls would sit and watch him battle. I was invited to their fight club one evening. Since they knew Shaadi was my aunt, they all had a special regard for me.

He tried to make fun of our group that night, and he wondered why they let a skinny girl order them around. I had previously assured Shaadi that I would avoid getting into any mischief.

That night, I went back on my word and begged him to fight beside me! He thought I was joking at first, but when he saw me warming up and getting ready, he sent his boy to tell me that I should sit and watch like the other girls since he didn't want to hurt me!

We were being watched by about fifty lads and females. I didn't want to give up as I always do, so I yelled and said, "If you don't play, the game will be mine!"

He came and said he didn't know where to begin and that he was afraid of my aunt and that if he didn't, he'd kick me! I started by punching him in the gut! Then I noticed a girl who had scribbled on a large cardboard, "LET HIM WIN," from afar.

I ignored it because I assumed it was one of his lovers. He was exhausted after ten minutes, so I delivered the last blow!

He fell and couldn't get back up! I was convinced he was faking it, but he wasn't. He was brought to the hospital after an ambulance was dispatched. I felt irritated with myself for not quitting.

I sat on the bench, perplexed. "He had a brain tumor," said the same girl who was holding the board before.

I was so inebriated that I didn't even realize what I was doing! After three weeks, that boy passed away!

During those three weeks, I began reading everything I could about the brain tumor, its stages, and treatment options. I even begged Shaadi to support the family economically, but that didn't work out!

This is another tragic fact of my life, and it has provided me with a wealth of information on tumors, which I now understand why! Still, I couldn't forgive myself; shame follows me everywhere!

I told Albert that what goes around comes around! So this is what's going on right now; his family has never forgiven me! This is my destiny coming back to haunt me.

Then we both became silent for a time, lost in our own worlds, until Albert announced that he would be departing in the evening because his father wanted him to attend one of his cousin's weddings.

He was curious about my plans. I just informed him that I would begin treatment and, if necessary, surgery.

Albert sat near the waterfall on the edge of a seat and said, "He needs to tell me something before anyone else!" I assured him that it couldn't be any worse than what doctor had just told me, so please continue.

He told out that, due to my health, I might never get another chance to fly, therefore any thoughts of becoming a pilot should be put on hold or just let go.

But he wanted me to be his personal pilot for his own plane, so I could travel anywhere he went and he could get everything he wanted! Certainly, but he was very thoughtful.

I informed him that dreaming of flying would always exist, but being a genuine pilot was not my purpose, thus not becoming a real pilot isn't a big concern for me, but Shaadi will have a heart attack if she finds out! Anyway, I hugged him and told him to let me know if flying at my stage was safe!

Then he turned the subject to his seven-day wedding and the numerous ceremonies he and his wife performed to thank the guests and royals who had traveled from all over the world!

Because I was tired, I asked if I might go to my room and rest; he led me to my room and then left, saying, "Please be fine until my next visit!"

Sir Malik had surprised us by inviting a bunch of musicians to perform Natural's favorite tune. He was such a big lover, so this was a huge surprise. Natural leapt into the air and kissed him.

What a lovely song she had requested, so ancient and classic.

Natural wasn't in the spirit to resume her tale that day; she rather to spend her time with her adoring hubby!

They insisted on my staying, as was customary, but I didn't want to bother these two lovers. I contacted my father, who was fortunately still at the hotel, and asked him to get ready to go out for dinner.

I was thinking about Albert on the drive to the hotel, speculating how he may be dressed. or how many guards accompanied him too Natural? I wished I could meet him one day since I'm sure he has a fascinating story to tell!

That night, we went to a restaurant named the Hidden Beauty, which was located outside of the city.

It featured a spectacular view from the outside, and peacocks roamed freely throughout the restaurant's garden. It was fantastic.

We ordered steaks and received free ice cream, fresh juice, and a variety of other beverages in honor of Women's Day! I told my father that he was fortunate to have me with him because he should have paid for everything!

We returned to the hotel late at night, and the receptionist handed me a note from Sir Malik. He wanted to let me know that Natural won't be at home tomorrow, so he'd like to utilize his turn to tell the story, and he'd prefer to see me in the hotel lobby or conference room, with my father's consent!

# Chapter 12
# Darkness Grows

My father was overjoyed at the prospect of serving as a host for the day. Then he said he'd phone the hotel director in the morning and arrange a meeting room.

Everything was organized the next day, and he came at nine a.m. He was finally able to enter the conference room after meeting and greeting a few folks in the reception area. In case we both needed a break, I had already requested coffee, tea, and some light snacks.

He was quite satisfied with all of the preparations and apologized for causing us any inconvenience. He claimed that the last time he was alone in a house with a lady, he ended up marring her! He didn't want to make the same error twice!

We all chuckled, and I knew he wanted to honor Natural's feelings; it didn't take him long to get started, because he'd previously been informed by his lovely wife.

Sir Malik began in the following manner:

What occurred to me the day Natural departed my house is impossible to express! I didn't want to let her go because she was a part of me, but her aunt threatened to send the entire police station if I didn't let her go.

I had intended to inform Natural of my feelings for her. When I returned home and saw her in that state, I completely forgot about everything. I tried to persuade her to go to the hospital, but she hesitated!

I began to see that she was occasionally talking to herself, or that I could see that she had injured her arm, hand, or even her leg without realizing it! She was acting extremely differently from the day she arrived at my house; as a result, I didn't know everything about her and assumed it was all part of her personality! I could sense that she was going through a lot of changes, but she wasn't ready to tell me about them.

Some nights, I could hear noises downstairs, and the lights in her room and the antique room were turned on; at first, I assumed she was discreetly talking on the phone or maybe having a visitor! But later on, I realized it was all in her head!

I felt she had a personality condition after hearing her life narrative and everything she had been through!

I attempted to persuade myself that my sensations were caused solely by her being in my presence. Regrettably, I was at a loss for what to do.

Why were we both having trouble sharing a meaningful conversation with each other? I'd never had somebody to talk to about anything, especially my emotion. I realized this was a test for me, and that the ideas I'd nurtured for years were about to crumble, since Natural was the only pearl in the ocean!

She took my heart with her the day she left the house, despite her deteriorating health. I went insane, didn't eat or drink for days till Jamal came home and offered to assist me in getting back on my feet.

He opened up and told me everything after I told him what Shaadi had requested me to do and how Natural was!

Natural and her love for me were discussed, as well as why she wanted to come to my location and work! Men aren't supposed to cry, but I proved them wrong.

I was too devastated to let go of my love and grieved a lot after learning everything!

Then I tried calling her, but my calls were either denied or not forwarded to her! I requested Jamal to pay her a visit, but Shaadi arranged false business travels to force him to fly alone to another city.

Days were passing me by, and I was in a romance with a lady I couldn't even seek out to, whether I wanted it or not!

All of my classes were canceled, and I stayed at home. I went to Shaadi's residence several times but was denied entry by the security.

Shaadi slammed the doors shut in my face!

I knew I'd let Natural down, so I wasn't expecting a call from her. Jamal phoned me from the hospital one day and told me about the factory explosion. He stated that if he could see these individuals and understand their misery, I could change my mind and begin to live again!

I chose to visit the hospital that day.

We went to the emergency ward, and they let us in because Jamal was known to the ward's administrator.

While I was occupied, I noticed Natural and her aunt coming to the scan ward! I initially mistook myself, but when I saw Jamal's astonished expression, I knew he had seen the same folks!

We were unable to see other areas of the hospital due to restrictions. Jamal vowed he'd figure out what they were up to. He returned a few days later with the tragic news of Natural's illness.

I was thinking that at this point in her life, she might want to spend time with the people she cares about so that they can emotionally shield and support her.

I was going insane and considered kidnapping her, but Jamal refused to help, saying he would try to break into the house in some way.

Sir needed a break, so I poured him some tea and offered him some cookies; he took a sip and decided to continue: I read in one of the local newspapers that Prince Albert was in town, and that was why her aunt didn't want us to be there.

At the same time, I was jealous and irritated. I began my search for someone who might deliver my message to the prince and request his assistance.

Natural had previously informed me that they were good friends, and that he might be able to grasp the problem and assist me, but getting to the prince was another challenge for an average guy like me.

I just had one objective in life at the time, which was to reclaim my love!

I discovered a bag full of infant items in Natural's room one night when I was trying to get Prince Albert's address or private phone number.

I assumed they were to Natural's childhood and that her mother had saved them for her, although she seemed a little wired while carrying them. I couldn't understand out why she was asking for help, or even carrying a bag full of baby items! I informed Jamal about it and showed him the note! He was confident it had not been written with a pencil or pen; it had been written with blood!

I was agitated, wondering why Jamal had known about her for so long and had remained silent. Every day, I asked him the same question; he knew everything there was to know about her, and if he had informed me, so many things would have been avoided, but I couldn't resist fate.

I received a call from the police station one evening, instructing me to attend there right away!

Shaadi was upset because I was upsetting her niece!

They planned on keeping me for the night.

I dialed Jamal's number, and he arrived with a lawyer and released me!

As much as she was fighting me back, it was making me more certain, not to give up. She wanted to show me her power and money. She was mistaken, I was after Natural and couldn't give up, till I got her back!

We were interrupted by the hotel owner, who wanted to take advantage of Sir Malik's celebrity and turn this visit into a promotional opportunity for the hotel!

Sir Malik, to my knowledge, was one of those who had never advertised for any channel or firm, so he declined, but said he would like to have tea with him.

Sir requested me to call my father in as well, and I knew this would be the end of the narrative with him!

He sat with my father and the hotel manager for another thirty minutes.

I was waiting for him in the lobby, trying to take in all of the information he provided me.

My mind was so preoccupied with what Sir Malik said today, that he mentioned a bag of infant clothes and a message, implying that Natural was not dreaming, that she was speaking the truth, but there were two ways to find out!

Sir Malik approached me and explained that he had been unable to complete the main part of his novel and that he would prefer Natural to finish it.

Many people waited in front of the hotel for Sir to arrive.

This was supposed to be a surprise visit, but the staff wasn't very adept at keeping secrets!

I spent the entire day writing.

I was up early the next day, intending to walk half-way to Sir's house, but my mind was preoccupied with the story, which slowed me down.

Sir slept while Natural was watering the plant. Sir appeared to be suffering from a severe headache and had been awake all night.

Because the weather was so nice, we decided to stay in the garden.

Usual Natural was busy making her tea set and pastries in anticipation of my arrival! She expressed regret for not having enough time to tell stories the day before.

She was more concerned for me and, in particular, my father, because it was because of them that we had left everything and traveled such a long distance to hear their story! I told her not to be concerned; in fact, my father was taking a break from his normal routine, and I had found exactly what I needed!

After a brief exchange, she began: It took me a few days to emerge from my cocoon. I was sick and heartbroken and I wasn't getting the love and protection I needed at the moment. I was absolutely ruined!

Shaadi came to see me more frequently than previously, but we had nothing in common.

One of the helpers, who used to be with me all the time, sent me a hidden note one of those days! She was terrified and requested that I keep a secret from Shaadi.

She said Jamal came, but she wouldn't let him visit you, so he asked me to deliver this letter to you!

I took her letter and walked to the bathroom, where I locked myself in!

It was Malik who wrote about everything, including Shaadi and how she is attempting to stop them, their phone call, and finally his sentiments!

That was the best of them all.

Let me read you the most important paragraph of his letter.

She then took out the envelope from a notebook she had opened. She only chose one of the four pages available.

**There was nothing but darkness in my universe until you arrived. I never believed in sorcery and instead emerged out of nowhere. It's not easy to discover love! If you feel it, don't be hesitant to convey how much importance your relationship adds to your life, like Jamal advised me!**

**I've spent my entire life trying to stay away from something that God has already given to humans: looooooove!**

**I tried holding on to my feelings and not giving up for years, but as I saw you, I forgot all about it! I didn't know what to call my sensation; at first, I mistook it for a habit, but it was much more!**

**I was absolutely crushed the day you left, and it was only then that I realized what I was feeling: love.**

**My beloved princes, I will not give up on you, and I implore you not to either.**

**I'll find a way, even if it takes some time. If you ever replace my smiles with someone else's, I'll be sad. If you gaze into the eyes of other guys, I will feel envious. If someone comes close to you, I'll go insane!**

**I'm sorry for letting you go from my grasp so quickly.**

**I had no idea how valuable you were until I had you, and now I can't even hear you!**

**I'm not promising you that it will be simple; I am promising you that it will be worthwhile.**

**Perhaps we are not destined to be together today, but rather in the future.**

**Someone once told me that if you've suffered enough to earn her, the right person will appear.**

**Please hold your horses till I arrive!**

**We'll get together again.**

**Yours, Malik.**

To me, the letter was significant.

I was overjoyed that he had figured it out! When he was penning the letter, I imagined his expression! The letter had a whiff of his cologne on it. I treasured it!

There was no one in the room when I exited the restroom. I pondered where I could stow the letter away from Shaadi's spies! Finally, in one of my mother's old purses, I found a home in my cupboard!

I couldn't figure out why Shaadi had become my biggest foe. What was it that she so desperately desired from me?

There was only one way to find out: I had to enlist Albert's assistance in my investigation!

I know she wasn't concerned about Albert's money; she was anxious about something else, and she wanted me to be separated from everyone and be with her!

My treatment began quite quickly. I was on a different kind of medication at the time, but it produced a variety of side effects and reactions on my body!

My walking was back to normal, with the exception of occasional limping, as the doctor changed them.

I was hesitant to phone Malik because I was afraid that if Shaadi found out, she would harm him. However, I contacted him in my own way, via letter, and it was my driver who assisted me!

I asked Shaadi if she had any news from Jamal when I returned from the hospital one night, and she answered no! I asked her if there was any reason, she didn't want to do business with him. She stated that knowing everything was not necessary; the most important thing was my health, and she needed to concentrate on that!

When I returned to my room later that night, I discovered a suitcase on my bed that I had left at Sir Malik's house. I assumed Jamal had arrived or had sent it through the driver, but when I queried the workers, they had no idea! When I unzipped the bag, the only thing I saw was a message that said "HELP."

When I turned around, I spotted her standing behind me! I was terrified; I thought her story and my nightmare had ended, but they had not.

I explained why she should give up: I even informed her that I knew she was on my mind, and it was time for her to leave, and I was unwell as a result of the stress! She suddenly snatched up a vase and tossed it out the window.

When the Scullery maid entered my room and spotted the damaged window, she immediately called Shaadi.

Not so long Everyone was in my room, questioning why I did that! Although the cursed girls were still around, I was the only one who could see her!

I apologized to Shaadi and requested that they vacate my room. She approached me and said that if I needed to talk to a psychologist, she knew one! She used to work with my mother as well!

She wanted me to see a psychologist right away, which was ridiculous! I told her I didn't have to, but I'd consider it! I believe she had been waiting for this opportunity to get something from me, and I showed her how.

Shaadi wanted one of her assistants to stay in the room with me after everyone had left, so I wouldn't harm myself!

The help stayed to follow Shaadi's orders, which caused the girl to leave me for a while, but she returned, and this time, I was in the toilet, she threw the bin in the mirror. As is customary, everything was reported to Shaadi, and she said she would make preparations for a doctor visit tomorrow!

I didn't know what to do; all those pills were also causing me to lose my sense of self. How could I describe all of it?

Who's going to trust me? Turley I was also tired of the way my mind worked; there was no more concealing. I suspected it was a side effect of the illness or simply something passed down to me from my MUM; now I was both mentally and physically struggling!

I didn't even eat that night since I wasn't hungry. I sat in the room and began reading Sir Malik's new book, which I had failed to finish the previous time.

What a lovely conclusion to his story! That night, it definitely took my mind off things, especially because the help was in my room all night! As I felt terrible for her, I let her lie on my bed while I read!

I intended to write Sir Malik a letter alerting him that I am having some troubles and will be seeing a psychotherapist, but I was hesitant to explain why!

I'm not sure why I was so terrified of My aunt's capabilities and what she could do with Malik. She was well aware that I had someone to look after!

The doctor came to our house the next day, Shaadi was in the room, and he requested if he may videotape the session. Shaadi wouldn't let him, saying, "Whatever is said here will stay here!"

The first thing he said to me was how much I resembled my mother!

That's something I get a lot, I told him!

He then inquired as to why I wanted to visit him in the first place. I told him it was Shaadi's idea, that she thought there was something wrong with me and that she wanted me to speak with you.

I also told him about Shaadi and my parents' relationship. When it came to love stories, I explained Sir Malik and what it was like to be him!

He wanted to know if I wanted to go back to acting like males or even dressing like them after Malik had put me down.

My response was self-evident; I chose to respect who I was and reclaim everything I had previously lost!

I didn't let him ask any more questions; it was now my turn to grill him!

I asked him to tell me about my mother and the problems she was having.

He initially objected, claiming that he couldn't discuss a patient's case with another person, but because she was dead and I was the daughter, he didn't see an issue!

He claimed that my mother was a sleepwalker, and that it started out as once or twice a month, then became every night, and that she was getting wounded if she was left alone!

"Your father was the one who tried to look after her, but things got out of his control on occasion. She once plunged into the pool and drowned herself, and another time she leaped off the balcony, breaking her arm but luckily the bedroom was on the ground floor!"

"When your father realized, he couldn't keep watching her at night, he hired a night nurse!"

I inquired as to how long she had been unwell. He stated "it had been over three years, and anytime she was anxious, this happened more frequently!"

That day, I had a lot of questions, such as what was causing my mother's concern. Why was she deteriorating instead than improving? What medication was she taking, who was her night nurse, and so on, but the doctor wouldn't answer any of them?

He stated that he is here to assist me in improving my health, not to discuss my mother's situation!

Before departing, he told Shaadi that he would like to see me again in his clinic. He needs to take a few tests from me, therefore it's much better for me to be there.

Shaadi was concerned that someone would notice me there, so she told that the day he would have me there, he would have to cancel the rest of his visits!

That day, I was truly missing my mother, and just thinking about her made me miss her even more!

Natural jumped up and stretched, then said, "It's almost two o'clock, let's wake Malik and go out for lunch!"

It took them half an hour to get ready, while I was jotting down my views on a piece of paper and recording them! Her mother's thoughts made me miss my own mother.

When I arrive to the hotel, I'm going to phone my own mother! Since my arrival, I haven't talked to her on the phone.

Sir didn't appear pleased to be leaving the house, but he had little option; there was no food!

We went to one of the city's classic restaurants; it didn't have a brand new design, but the food was delicious and fresh! Natural stated that she adores this location and that she will reveal why later!

We were all hungry, so catching our food didn't take long. I observed they didn't chat much at the table, so I made an effort and asked them whether they have any intention of remaining silent when they eat together.

Sir Malik said that they value and respect the cuisine, and that they are attempting to be appreciative!

I was inspired by their ideas!

Sir Malik dropped us off at our house and explained that he had to go to a chat show on one of the television stations.

Natural stated that now that her stomach is full, she will be able to speak more freely.

# Chapter 13
# Secrets Stollen

She jumped right in.

Albert showed up to our house the next day, seemingly out of nowhere. I was relieved to see his face this time because I had been so lonely! He arrived with a large number of gifts!

He reasoned that I could enjoy one of the gifts, and therefore he would gain access to my heart, if only for a short while!

The book written by Sir Malik was one of the nicest gifts I received!

I never heard of this book, and I didn't even know it existed!

He came and sat beside me on the ground in my room and said: I told you I will find a way to your heart through one of my presents!

He claimed that the government possessed this book because it dealt with political matters, and that it had never been published, and that it was written in your Malik's handwriting.

I yelled and hugged him, telling him how thrilled he had made me. I also told him I hoped he knew I had this copy with me!

Albert inquired if I had any communication with him, to which I replied that I did not!

He inquired as to why, and I told him about Shaadi, but not about what Sir Malik had written to me, only about her attitude toward me and Sir! I even told him about Jamal and how she had abruptly terminated her business ties with him!

Shaadi won't do anything without a reason, Albert remarked, laughing. Every action she performs is accompanied by a thorough explanation and, of course, an advantage!

Hearing those things about her astonished him! He claims that she always admits in their chats that you are the only family member she has left, and that whatever she has will one day be yours.

But to limit and prevent you from going about your daily routine is something fresh that I'm hearing right now!

I related what had happened the day before (without mentioning the girl of my nightmares), and I was also urged to see a doctor! He questioned, with a mournful expression, what she had forced you to do this time.

I didn't want to start a fight between Albert and Shaadi, so I quickly adjusted my comments and told him that she had done an excellent job for me.

At the very least, I'm able to communicate with others and express myself. His face had returned to normal when he shook his head in agreement.

Shaadi arrived in my room quickly. We were sitting on the ground, which shocked her. Albert said he was comfortable sitting in this position before she began her remarks.

She wanted us to go to the banquet hall so that they could feed us!

She exited the room once we complied. I told Albert not to say anything and to keep his mouth sealed!

At the table, I ate my diet meal, which had been prepared in secret. There were numerous medicines I should have taken after each meal, and I then spent an hour puking up everything I had eaten. Those drugs were making me feel much worse!

Albert had to leave the next day, but we agreed to meet in the evening in the garden outside of Shaadi's site.

I arrived late because I was throwing up in the bathroom, so I hurriedly washed and changed, since he was preparing to leave by the time I arrived!

I informed him of my lateness. He returned, sat near the fountain on a seat, and invited me to join him.

I noticed he was crying as he clutched my hand.

He informed me that he is afraid of losing me and that he wants to take me out of the jail that Shaadi had held me in!

He wrapped his hand around my waist and drew me in.

I was falling for all of those emotions as well, and I was about to give up everything and devote myself entirely to him, but the gardener's voice saved us!

When Albert requested me to accompany him to his room, I looked him in the eyes and informed him that this was all wrong and that we couldn't meet again if we continued to act in this manner!

He stated that all he wanted to do was kiss me!

I drew myself away from his arm and told him I needed him as a friend and that I adored Malik.

Please do not jeopardize our friendship.

He stated he travels thousands of miles every week to see me, so at the absolute least I get to kiss him as a simple thank you!

I considered him a friend, but I forgot that he is a guy with wants!

"Thousands of girls throw themselves at me for free," he continued, "but being with you is different." He's romantically entangled by me. My physique, my mind, my emotions, and my company are all on his wish list!

He claimed that he tolerated his wife's dishonesty because he was with me! As a result, anytime he comes to see me, he won't need to carry any excuses!

I stood up and took off my bathrobe, told him that if he came over tonight, I'd give him whatever he wanted! So, you won't have to travel quite as far next time!

He returned my bathrobe to me and informed me that I needed everything, not just your body, as I had stated, and then he began walking away with a sad face!

I sat on the seat and felt so warm on the inside that I believed no one could comprehend me at that time. I reasoned that at least I'd have someone to talk to in that prison, but he was preoccupied with his own demands.

I'm not sure how long I sat there because my legs couldn't move. I got to my feet, but I couldn't keep my balance. I knew I was in trouble at the moment, and the stress was exacerbating the situation.

When I called for assistance, the same gardener rushed over, holding my hand as I stood up; sadly, one person was insufficient to lift me!

He requested that I wait while he summoned further assistance.

I was transported to my room after a while, but there was no sign from Shaadi or Albert...

My medication was handed to me by the staff. I asked her if she could bring the phone to my bedside, and she said she would, but she has been ordered to report any calls made from my room to Madam Shaadi!

I was going to phone Malik only to hear his voice, completely disregarding my personal boundaries!

She then went outside and stood guard at the door, ensuring that no one entered!

I dialed Sir Malik's number somewhere after midnight, and he didn't respond right away.

He responded with a drowsy voice when I called again.

I remained silent and let him to continue speaking... Before I hung up, he asked, "Is that you, Natural?" He stated that he can sense my presence! He also stated that he missed me!

I was speechless and crying just hearing to his voice!

Then I hung up the phone! Having heard his voice felt like paradise; it was like a pain reliever!

Tessa, the helper's name, inquired as to why I had not spoken to him. I explained how much I missed his voice and that I didn't want to offend him.

She stated that she had read practically all of Sir Malik's novels and wished to see him in person one day!

I told him he was coming last Christmas, but I believe she wasn't permitted to come amongst the guests, so she couldn't see him.

Tessa claimed that everyone in the house was talking about him and how attractive he is, as well as how he was admiring you the entire night!

We're both very lucky to have found each other, she said. She prayed for us and requested the Lord to help me get healthy so that I may return to him!

It was wonderful to hear her, and like a small girl, I clutched her hand while she spoke, and promptly dozed off!

The next morning, I awoke to the sound of a doctor's voice, and Shaadi stood behind him! Do I know what time it is? he said as he grasped my hand. He inquired whether I knew which day it was after I informed him it might be afternoon. I told him Wednesday would be the most likely date.

He informed me that I had been sleeping without food or water for the last two days! He was not sure how I did it!

He motioned for me to leave my bed. I tried to move my body, but I couldn't since I had an IV in my hand!

Albert left the next day, according to Shaadi, but he has been phoning every day simply to hear my voice!

My aunt was so worried about Albert that I didn't answer his calls.

Now that I'm awake, the doctor says he needs to take me to the hospital and perform another scan.

I inquired if that was necessary, and he replied that if it wasn't, he wouldn't bother me in this state!

So, while others were outside getting ready, Tessa whispered into my ear that Sir Malik had sent two letters!

I quickly requested that she hand them over to me, and then I began reading them. One of them was the first chapter of his new book, in which I played the lead role! I was overjoyed; I couldn't think he'd write about me one day!

In the other letter, he requested that I meet him on Friday in a downtown restaurant.

When I asked Tessa what day it was today, she responded Friday, and it was already afternoon! I let out a shriek. She inquired as to why I am tense.

I handed her the letter, and she said she'd arrange for the driver to meet Sir Malik there and inform him of your condition.

I assured her I was going to make it today no matter what! That could be my last chance to see him, and there was no way I was going to blow it. I urged Tessa to devise a strategy, and we managed to dodge Shaadi.

The only way she won't attend, she claimed, is to fabricate a phony tale about one of her firms and have the driver phone her and tell her to be there at that location.

We both burst out laughing, which was a good thing because the only way Shaadi would have given up was if she had something to do with her money!

She returned after a few moments and confirmed the call had been completed!

Shaadi summoned us to come down, but there had been no cancellation from her end yet.

Because I was having trouble moving, Shaadi requested the helpers to arrange one of the rooms downstairs for me.

She approached me and took my hand in hers, inviting me to sit in a chair for a bit!

Then her phone rang, she stepped away for a moment, returned with a distressed expression on her face, and explained that something serious had arisen, and no one else could help except her!

So she wanted me to go to the doctor with Tessa and the driver, and she said she'd wait for me to return!

We were all relieved that the plan had gone off without a hitch.

My scan was completed as soon as I arrived at the hospital, and we quickly left, instructing the driver to transport me to the location Malik requested.

When we arrived, the driver first checked to see if Sir Malik was still there, then returned with a smile on his face and said, "He's still waiting!"

I told Tessa that she had been longing for this time to meet Sir Malik. She's welcome to accompany me, and I'll present her to him as a friend!

She was overjoyed and repeatedly kissed me.

My pulse was racing, I was nervous to meet him, and I wasn't the same Natural he remembered. I came to a halt and glanced at Tessa, who saw my anxious expression and said, "Mam, we've gone so far, can't give up!"

She was correct; I forced myself to walk, and once he spotted me, he couldn't figure out how to come closer to me! He approached me and took my hand before telling Tessa, "I've got her now, don't worry!"

He then led us to his table.

I introduced Tessa to him and told him how much of a friend she is and how she goes to such lengths to help us. Malik stepped up and shook her hand, thanked her, invited her to join us, and asked if she would wait in the car because she was so shy!

Natural explained to me, "Now you understand why the restaurant where we ate today was so valuable!" It was the same establishment! This was where Malik and I had our first cover up date!

"I had a feeling there was a backstory." I took the initiative to speak.

Since she was going to the kitchen, she inquired if I needed anything. I thanked her and informed her that I needed to hear what had transpired in the restaurant before going home because I needed to shut off my mind before going to bed!

She promised to return soon.

She made a start.

Malik had changed drastically, he now had gray hair and was quite skinny. When I inquired, he stated that the day I left was his last day of living, and then he proceeded to tell me the entire tale.

We didn't have much time, so I could only tell him about my and Albert's arguments! I was feeling bad about myself. I had to inform him!

He told me he respects me even more now than before, so don't think of these things!

I told him we should run away, but he refused; instead, he insisted on being a gentleman and coming to pick me up as his bride!

I couldn't believe what he said, so I asked him to repeat himself. He said he wants me to be his wife and that he won't run away.

When he realized I was nervous, he took my hand in his and whispered, "I knew you were mine from the beginning."

I tried to ignore you, but I couldn't; it was impossible; it was like a terrible obsession!

He kissed my hand and apologized for making a decision without consulting me; I didn't ask you whether you wanted to marry me, and I won't... Even if you say no, it's too late because you're mine!

At that time, I was in tears. He tried to calm me down by hugging me. I addressed him by his first name, and he refused to let me continue, saying, "Please say my name again, Malik."

He admitted that it was the first time I mentioned his name without using the word "SIR."

I requested him to take a good look at me. I'm no longer a pilot, nor am I a gorgeous, sporty, red-haired lady who could beat him in a football game!

Now, I'm not any of those things; I'm just as sick as ever and will soon be in a wheelchair; don't you think you should take your time and not rush it?

Malik kissed my palm and said he hadn't noticed I'd changed, that I was still a lovely, attention-getting woman with a magnificent talent!

He's stated that he'd like to be beside me.

He said that he had been summoned to the police station in the morning, but that it had nothing to do with Shaadi!

I inquired as to how he knew this. Then he went on to ask if I remembered those of his pupils who had died in an accident, as he had shown me in the papers. Yes, I confessed.

I took a peek…

You don't trust me when I say what I saw?

It turned out to be her. My dream's narrator! I first assumed I was mistaken and examined the situation more closely. It turned out to be her.

Tessa arrived at the same time and stated, "It's too late; madam Shaadi will send her people to find us!" Malik didn't seem to realize that I was speechless.

Malik tightened his grip on my hand and whispered, "We'll meet again soon!"

"Jamal has some ideas," he said, "and I will discover about them soon!"

I couldn't understand a word he said! I was aware that he was still speaking, but as my body began to sweat, they both assisted me in getting to the car! When I glanced at him as the car drove away, I had a slight feeling that I wouldn't see him again!

Tessa was concerned, and she inquired as to why I was so quiet. Why was my skin so pale? I simply closed my eyes and told her I was exhausted and needed to sleep!

I was thinking about what I saw in the newspaper as I drove. I had been unsure about my visions for a long time, but after seeing the newspaper, I was confident about her!

She was real, but who was she and why did she want to track me down? I had no idea what her name was!

I wish I had known about this when I was already in Sir's place, so I could have taken action! I couldn't accomplish anything because of my current state.

Unfortunately, in Shaadi's hands, I was like a piece of clay!

Shaadi was waiting for us and asked Tessa why we were so late?

I told her I was lonely and insisted on having the driver take me all over the city!

She expressed her hope that everything I've been saying is correct!

"My results will be ready in the evening, and the doctor will come and talk to us about them!"

She expressed herself.

I praised her for her thoughtfulness! Then I requested Tessa to assist me in getting to my new room on the bottom floor. The room featured a unique style, resembling one of those hotel suits, complete with a plethora of gift bags.

Tessa assisted me in taking a quick shower, then I requested her to wake me up in one hour!

My eyes felt heavy, and I wasn't sure if it was a side effect of the drug or anything else, but soon I was in bed, I was out!

I awoke early so that I could be ready when the doctor arrived! When he arrived, he had a very sorrowful expression on his face.

We headed to the meeting room as usual, but this time it was just me, Shaadi! The tumor has shifted and is now in a dangerous spot, according to the doctor, and the only option now is operations.

I was thinking to myself about how quickly my life was changing; everything was happening quickly! That day, I received two shocking pieces of information!

Shaadi didn't seem astonished; she had been expecting my response! I recall the first time the doctor informed Albert of my illness and how she tried to show sympathy.

How could it have grown or moved that quickly, I asked? Everything I was told had been done to the letter!

Instead, than looking at me, the doctor turned to Shaadi and said, "We can't predict everything!"

So it was up to me to make the decision, with no alternatives offered!

If it weren't for Malik, I would have accepted the death and let things end in peace!

I couldn't risk losing my chance to be with Malik, so I knew I had to get the operation, but I still needed to know how long we'd have to wait!

Doctor stated he wasn't sure, but it might be less than 10 days!

We all exited the conference room at the same moment, and I motioned for Tessa to accompany me to the Garden, which she did. It was dark, but I wanted some fresh air!

I proceeded to my own area beside the fountain, which I hadn't been since Albert! Oh, he's gone! Where did his feelings and affection for me go? I was just thinking about that.

Tessa had been asked to leave me alone for a time. I'll sit far away and wait for my call, she remarked.

Natural went to answer the phone as soon as we heard it ring; it was my father on the other end. Because it was late, he wanted to know whether I needed him to pick me up.

Natural apologized and stated that since Sir was not yet home, she would phone for their driver and see that I arrived safely at the hotel!

She dialed a driver's number right after my father's call and requested him to come right away! She approached me, but I refused to let her apologize. I informed her that I was the one who was eager to learn more!

She requested me to accompany her to their storage room in the back garden before I left. She pulled out an old suitcase and asked, "Do you know what this is?"

I had no idea what it was, and I was hoping she would tell me! So, after I shook my head as a sign of No, she opened it and found it full of infant clothes!

Sir Malik, she conceded, knows nothing about them! He thinks I threw them away, but I wanted to create our story and save all the proof for the person who will be our novelist, and then I'll trash them!

I assured her that I would have believed her anyhow, and that she didn't have to keep them! She took it out of the storage and walked with me to the gate, where she placed it next to the large bin outside!

We said our goodbyes, she looked cheerful, and the driver arrived on time.

That night, I ended up writing until the morning. Something was keeping me up at night, and I had a sneaking suspicion that something was off in the story... I was making educated guesses about the alternatives!

# Chapter 14
# The Unforgettable

We intended to walk to the lobby after breakfast and noticed Natural there.

She claimed she was too bored to stay at home and felt isolated, so she decided to do something different today after Sir Malik departed for work. did the right thing, I told her.

Then she begged my father's permission to take me somewhere with her! My father didn't mind; all he asked was for her to let him know when I'd be back.

Natural scribbled my father's address and phone number on a piece of paper and told him he may call whenever he wanted.

I didn't want to keep inquiring about where we were going, so I decided to wait and see what Natural had planned for us today!

It took us twenty minutes to get to that location, which happened to be a psychological clinic!

Natural grinned and said, "A little bit more, and then you'll see the biggest surprise!"

Although there were several structures, the driver knew exactly where to go. We both got down, and Neutral requested that the driver waits for us till we returned!

Natural was recognized by Security, and he greeted us warmly. Then one of the nurses met us and led us to a particular room, where everything was set up and cleaned, but there appeared to be no one living there!

There was a dining table in the center of the room, a closet in one corner, and a little bed in the other, but there was no trace of a washroom.

Natural informed the Nurse that she had spoken with their supervisor and that the room had been reserved for us for the day.

She then requested that I call my father and inform him of our location!

I did the exact same thing and left a message at the front desk!

We took our seats at the table, and the nurse exited the room as well. Natural inhaled deeply and got to work!

I didn't have a choice but to get surgery. The next day, I wrote Malik a letter in which I informed him of my surgical plans as well as the reasons for them.

Before, there was something I really wanted to do, and that was see my psychiatrist! When I told Shaadi, she smiled and stated, "I'm glad you've accepted your condition and are attempting to improve yourself!"

I went to see the doctor, at the psychologist clinic later that day. He had a completely different mentality this time, didn't address any of my inquiries, and kept asking me whether I had considered self-harm or suicide!

I simply disregarded him and told him that these were inappropriate inquiries, and he informed me that he had also obtained the records from the prior time I was admitted to the hospital.

In the occasion when I cut my feet on glass, the report stated that I did it to myself due to carelessness or lack of concentration!

Then he revealed that my aunt had informed him that I had tried to starve myself at one point!

I became so enraged that I informed him what he was attempting to demonstrate!

What purpose did he serve by fabricating these lies? I was being taped by him! That's why he insisted on meeting me at his office, I believe!

That day, I learned that he would no longer assist me. The only thing I did was remain silent and request that he contact my driver!

Shaadi was nowhere to be seen when I returned home. I dashed to my room and dialed Malik's number, but he was not at home.

I considered calling Jamal, but wasn't sure if he was with my aunt.

Then I sat down on my bed and began to pray.

I was terrified of surgery, yet it was the only way to stay alive at the moment! I was urged to keep using the wheelchair so that I might gain control and avoid injuring myself.

I just got a call from Albert, who claimed he owed me an apology and that he had heard about the surgery, but he couldn't forgive himself because he was the cause of the second shock!

This is my destiny, I remarked, and no one is to blame! So there's no need to be concerned. He explained that his father is ill, and that until he recovers, he should be the one to undertake all of the responsibilities because they are awaiting him! He won't be able to help me because of this!

I encouraged him not to be too hard on himself; everything would be fine. I also told him that if I survived surgery, I would love to return to the same island we had visited previously! We both said our goodbyes!

My aunt sat next to me at the dining table. She told me about her pregnancy, which she had never told me before!

My father rapidly planned to arrange for the wedding and get rid of me after learning about her relationship with their neighbor, she added.

She was, however, already the mother of a child. They had mistreated her in those days and threatened to take the kid away from her. The family waited till the child was born before giving it away!

I was so astonished that she was trying to talk to me right now; I assumed she was trying to be pleasant because she believes I will never recover from that surgery!

I couldn't ask any questions since I was too astonished; all I could do was tell her. Please accept my apologies for the events of the past.

She turned to face me and stated, "No one is born to be nasty; my father was simply trained to be this way!"

I inquired as to where the infant had been removed and to whom it had been handed.

She claimed that after searching for her for several years, she had finally found her. She was already a teenager, but she gave it her all, refusing to recognize her as her mother!

The Natural took a breather and explained why I hadn't asked her about this location. I told her that I'd learned not to spoil my surprises, especially when it comes to things or people I care about!

That, she said, was a wise decision! She then picked up the phone and dialed the coffee shop's number to have some refreshments sent to us!

After having our coffee which tasted terrible, she continued!

Knowing about Shaadi's daughter was one of the many surprises in my life. She claimed that her daughter had discovered her previously, but that she had no desire to know her!

I inquired about her identity. She grinned and added, "Her name is Elizabeth," which she had chosen for her, but she was confident that whoever kept her would change it as well!

"I'm sure she's prettier than her name," I said.

She affirmed that she had been missing for a long time by shaking her head! with a pained expression on her face.

Shaadi stated that she has looked everywhere for her and has found no trace of her! She hopes she isn't escaping!

She also revealed that she knows who is to blame, and that person will be apprehended shortly in order to assist her daughter in her disappearance.

Tessa was then instructed to phone the hospital and leave a message for my surgeon!

We ate in quiet, and we were both thinking the same thoughts!

She communicated with the doctor once he returned from the hospital and confirmed everything on my behalf. The earliest appointment was two days later!

Then she hung up and told me that I needed to modify the dose of my meds to what the Surgeon requested, and that he would send the new prescriptions!

I tried calling Malik again later that night, but he had not yet returned home! If something had happened to him, I was worried!

I have no recollection of the last two days I spent in bed.

They were administering several medications to me that made me drowsy.

The surgery day has arrived. I was escorted to the ward, but Shaadi didn't show up since she had left a note for Tessa, and she doesn't have the heart to see anything.

"Mam, I'm sorry I couldn't assist you; Mam, I'm sorry I couldn't stop them!" Tessa took my hand in hers and said, "Mam, I'm sorry I couldn't stop them!"

The doctor then came in and took me in!

She came to a halt in her narration, and I noticed her hands were quivering and her face was pale!

I quickly poured water into a glass for her! She drank a swig!

I told her that was enough for today; the narrative and the surroundings were stressing her out!

She stated that she must do so; she cannot leave the hospital until she has completed this dreadful chapter of her life!

"This has been causing me misery for years; I need to get it out of my chest!"

I begged her to unwind a little and promised her that I would not leave until she was finished!

I also advised her to stop if she felt anxious. There is no need to rush!

I was in the recovery room as soon as I awoke! I guess it had been two or three days since I had been in bed.

My arms were shackled to the bed as I strained to reach out of my skull. When a nurse entered, she instructed me to relax and called for a doctor!

Then the entire crew entered the room, and the doctor carefully pulled the tube from my mouth and slowly releasing my hand!

They then handed me a little glass of warm water and instructed me to rinse my lips with it! The nurse then handed me a mirror and instructed me to examine myself.

Unfortunately, my entire head was shaved and wrapped in a large bandage! When I asked for my surgeon, nurse said he had gone to a bigger hospital in city for an emergency!

Shaadi came to see me the next day! She stated that the surgery was a complete success and that I would be OK in no time!

The room was brimming with the flowers from Albert.

How many days have I been in the hospital? I wondered aloud. What if Malik sent me a letter or attempted to phone me while I was in the hospital?

Then I convinced myself that it was better that he wasn't present to witness my predicament. All of my beauty was gone, and I was in a wheelchair with a shaved head!

Shaad stated that if everything goes well, I will be released soon.

She also stated that the psychologist will visit me tomorrow, despite the fact that my last session with him did not go well.

I told Shaadi about what he said to me at his clinic the last time! She explained, "I'm in the early stages of mental illness, and the sooner I get rid of it, the better!"

Don't make me meet him, I told her.

She explained that because I come from a family of people with mental problems, she won't be able to help me until the situation on the other hand improves!

She also admitted to interacting with me psychologically throughout my youth.

She's no longer capable of lying!

I've hated my name, gender, and blamed myself for my parents' deaths my entire life!

"All of this has culminated in today's date; she should have taken me to the mental hospital sooner, but she delayed, and that is her fault," Shaadi explained.

My aunt had transformed into a stranger, unable to hear or see me and desperate to be free of me.

They were giving me pain relievers that made me so tired! The Psychologist arrived and confirmed what Shaadi had informed me the day before!

It was pointless to free myself from their clutches because I knew there was something wrong with me as well, seeing as that girl (ghost) was the epitome of it!

All the doors were shut in my face, and the only option was death!

After a few days, I was admitted to a mental institution for treatment. This is the room to which I was taken directly from the hospital.

I was in such a sour position!

I was being transported from the psychological hospital to the municipal hospital for a normal check-up and return!

There was no longer a home; Shaadi only came once or twice for a visit, and the rest of the days were spent with just me and my servants!

I asked Shaadi whether Tessa could come here and be with me, and she said that she had been stealing from us all this time, so she had asked her to quit!

This room had no phone, no TV, and no outside connections when I was there!

I requested if they could at least give me some books, and one of the employees, who was a little gentler than the rest, brought me Malik's books, and that was it!

My entire life consisted of reading and holding books in my arms till I fell asleep.

When I imagined Sir Malik being in front of me, they told me I was hallucinating when I spoke with him.

I have no idea what day of the week it was!

I saw her again one of those nights! She was in the hospital! She was upset and expressed her regret to me via hand signals.

She was clutching a piece of paper in her palm, and I informed her that she shouldn't approach me for help because I couldn't!

She didn't let go of the paper I was holding. When I opened it, the only word I noticed was "Believe."

She reminded me that I had lost faith. I'd entirely surrendered to the world's attraction.

I got out of bed and began praying, despite the fact that it was still difficult for me to bend.

No one bothered to let you know that there is still hope in this location, but suddenly a ghost will appear to remind you!

Then she turned to face me and whispered, "Only God knows how much I went suffering, how alone I was!"

Then she told me to join her on a walk so she could show me around! Do you believe this hospital was once home to the country's first female pilot? Everything was provided to me at one moment in my life, and then was turned upside down the next!

We lingered for another fifteen minutes, chatting with other nurses and patients, before departing!

Natural's hands were still shivering, so I inquired whether she was okay. She said that this is a result of my golden years and all those medications. It appears on occasion.

Natural told the nurse before she left that she would volunteer and pay for those who were in need!

The nurse hugged Natural and advised her to let the past be in the past, to be a free bird, to grasp her husband's hand and enjoy the rest of her life, and to never look back!

I took her hand in mine and told her, "I can't pretend I understand what's happened to her, or even feel what she's been through, but I'm confident the senior nurse was correct, and all she had to do now was look forward!"

She explained that this was another item she was saving to show me! She wanted me to see what she had gone through as well.

She invited me to go shopping with her, but I hesitated because I knew my father would be concerned if I didn't return on time!

They took me to the hotel. Natural remained depressed... I inquired if she had anything she wanted to share with me.

She explained that it is preferable that Sir Malik handle this part of the story since she would not be capable of delivering it to me appropriately if she remembered them! This is bad for her health!

She wanted me to go to their house tomorrow, so she'll be there as well, busy with other household duties!

# Chapter 15
# At A Loose Ends

I arrived late to Sir's house the next day because my father was sick with a cold, and I should have double-checked everything before leaving.

Sir was waiting for me, and once I explained why, he said he hoped he could cover practically the entire narrative because staying away from my family and in a hotel was not fair to me.

I told him not to worry about it because I needed to go back to the hotel as soon as possible. If we could start earlier, that would be preferable.

Natural arrived and offered us tea, explaining that she would continue to phone the hotel to inquire about my father's health and that she would prepare some nutritious meals, including soup, for me to take to him.

I apologized for causing her any inconvenience.

We decided to sit in the hall, which had practically all of Sir's artwork on the walls.

Sir had constructed stunning works of art, and I couldn't take my gaze away from them.

It took a long time for me to be able to concentrate on the story each time I was in the hall.

Sir noticed me glancing around and asked if I wanted an interdiction, which I readily accepted!

He spoke about his artwork as if it were a whole new book! There are so many details that I don't think anyone will see them. Why doesn't he write a tiny message for each? I inquired.

He liked the concept.

We both returned to the couch after a little while. He admitted that this aspect of the story is difficult for him as well, but that he cannot delegate it to Natural.

Sir confessed that the relationship with Natural had been severed at that point. Shaadi fired the driver and requested Tessa to leave since she had a feeling it had something to do with me.

Jamal was dispatched to another nation to handle her business, leaving me with nothing.

I felt I'd absolutely lost Natural at that moment!

Regrettably, I was also being investigated for a crime! One of my students had mysteriously disappeared, and the last place she had been seen was at my house!

I've been summoned to attend to the police station several times, and officers were also watching my house!

I used to have three pupils who came in for private lessons.

They were eighteen or nineteen-year-old buddies, two ladies and one gentleman.

Samuel, the rich boy, had a girlfriend named Natasha, who was friends with Pleasure, and they used to meet together for lessons.

They were outstanding among my other students and completely capable of producing new work on their own, especially with Pleasure.

The lesson started at seven in the evening that day, and not only Natasha but also Samuel and Pleasure were present. I gave them a project to do after an hour of instruction.

They were usually allowed to come to my house and begin their assignment and collaborate as a group.

Even if I had to go somewhere, I used to leave them alone.

I'm not sure why, but I placed my faith in them.

Jamal had a difficulty with his car on the same day, and it was entirely destroyed. He requested my assistance.

I left the two in my house alone ( Samuel and Pleasure).

Unfortunately, I returned late that night I was to weary to notice the unusual odor, which smelled like burning food or plastic.

The first thing that came to me was that it could have been some burned food.

I didn't see them in class after that day, none of them. Until I saw their pictures in the newspaper one day.

Samuel and Natasha were killed in a car accident due to excessive speed on the same night he held a class at my house.

He left and went to pick up his girlfriend (Natasha was his girlfriend). They had an altercation as usual, and he lost control, according to what I was told at the police station.

Natasha and Samuel had been arguing in my class for the past few sessions, but it was not my place to find out what they were fighting about.

Unfortunately, Pleasure went missing the same night, so the cops had reason to keep a watch on me. Their only suspicion was me.

All of my movements were monitored, and I was afraid to even walk outside Shaadi's palace because she had previously complained about me too! The cops had plenty of reasons to distrust me.

They had complete control over my phone calls.

I only knew Jamal through one of our mutual pals. Natural's medical records in the city hospital, according to Jamal, can help us track her down.

Natural was escorted from the Psychology hospital every Monday and would be returned to the same location following a check-up in the main hospital.

There is no one else with her but the nurse, who we are not allowed to speak with!

Natural was brought straight to a psychological hospital after having surgery... I could tell something wasn't quite right.

Jamal was out of Shaadi's sight at the time, on emergency leave; he was stunned as well.

Jamal's hospital friend informed us that if we were family, we could get a second opinion and even make a lawsuit, but because we aren't, he couldn't help us.

We were both looking for a method to help Natural, and Jamal was certain that everything that had happened to her was under Shaadi's control. Nothing could happen until she was aware of it.

I asked if we could speak with Albert to see if he could assist us. I was convinced that if we were able to explain her situation to him, he would take action!

The biggest issue was getting close enough to Albert!

So we spent two more days attempting to connect with Albert in various ways. According to Jamal, the most important relationship right now is who is looking after the palace's lower ranks.

We discovered a male worker in Shaadi's kitchen who was able to locate Albert's private phone number through his cousin, who worked in the castle's stable.

Amazing! Isn't that incredible? She had inquired of me.

Finally, we obtained the phone number, and Jamal took over and told him the complete story. He almost begged him to keep Shaadi out of the situation.

Prince Albert didn't take long to collect the information for us, although he justified himself for not becoming involved due to his position.

He stated that he will be king soon and that he does not want any misleading information to reach the public.

He connected us to one of the investigators who worked for VIP clients and assured us that we could trust him.

"I need to check on Natural," Sir Malik stated abruptly, "I don't like her to sit and dwell about the past."

"She's been going back in time a lot since we started narrating our journey,"

"She can't sleep at night anymore, especially when it gets to this part where she was alone in the hospital in that situation!"

I went to see Natural alongside him. She was reading a book as she sat by the pool.

She inquired as to whether or not we had completed the story. "No honey, there's still a long way to go!" Sir Malik responded, smiling.

Natural offered us lemonade.

She asked if I could assist her with watering the plant.

That pleased me, and it diverted my attention away from the plot for a moment.

Sir asked if I wanted to return to the hall, and I said yes. I didn't want to miss out on my chance to gaze at the paintings!

We returned to the same location as before, and he continued: "I was under police control, so the only one who could go to the investigator was Jamal; luckily, Shaadi was still convinced he was working in a foreign nation!"

He was one of the country's most expensive private detectives. Albert had already spoken with him and informed him that he is responsible for all charges and that he is also financially supporting us.

He began his inquiry from the hospital, and Jamal returned to his job before Shaadi learned of his absence!

The detective had his own employees all over the world, and I was the one who called him whenever I could get away from the cops. I was going to any shop and asking for a call!

When I initially contacted him, he told me that everything that happened to Natural was my responsibility, I didn't get him that time.

All of the hospital paperwork were not legal, and the doctor who diagnosed Natural had his license suspended two years ago as he was using someone else's name!

Natural was a completely healthy. He informed me.

The drugs she was given, which made her muscles lethargic and lazy, were generally given to animals!

She would literally lose her senses in her legs and other muscles in her body, because the brain tumor was not real and was made up at Shaadi's request!

I stood up and told Sir that she was the one who had done all of that to Natural!

What kind of person could be so heinous?

Then I began to cry, and Sir abruptly ended the story because of me. In structed me to keep my emotions in check and to be tough since I would be the one to tell the others about their tale.

I tried to calm down, but my tears wouldn't stop, so I told Sir to keep going and I'd be OK.

'Picture how you're feeling, and then imagine how she'd feel if she'd found out the complete story?' Sir Malik asked.

"How could he be so sure?" I inquired of the detective. When you have a lot of money, he added, you could purchase people.

Albert backed him financially, and he quadrupled the fee for everyone willing to speak for the Natural Case!

The police came to my house one day and searched everything thoroughly. What were they looking for? I have no idea! They asked where I'd stashed her?

Who was it that I had approached? Pleasure! the cops said.

I was asked to sign certain documents for them once they were finished before departing.

I went through the rest of the papers and discovered that the Missing girl's mother had filed a complaint.

### Margarete Shaadi Williams!

Again, I was taken aback! I thought I'd have a heart attack by the end of the story.

Sir smiled at me and remarked, "Don't get too enthusiastic! We still have a long way to go!"

After the police had departed, I went outside and found a location to phone Jamal, already told him that Shaadi was the one who had filed a report about her missing daughter! Jamal told me a few years ago that she had told him about finding her daughter in one of the orphanages!

She had informed him that her daughter was suffering from biological issues that he was unaware of!

Pleasure had also refused to live with her mother, according to Jamal.

Shaadi didn't want anyone to know about her secret because she was too young to be pregnant, and her child's father was missing.

She was never married to him, and her family forced her to marry one of the richest businessman's sons, after the birth of the child!

Jamal said to me that she always blamed Natural's father for everything!

He also claimed that Pleasure was apparently under Shaadi's watchful eye, with someone following her wherever she went. She was last spotted in my residence, sadly!

On my second contact to the detective, he informed me that Natural had been admitted to a psychology facility for a personality disorder.

Another reason she has been exploited is because she lost her parents at an early age. Her mother, it appeared, was also suffering from mental problems.

This has persuaded him to seek professional help. He is perplexed by Shaadi's threat that if he does not come up with an urgent case, she will murder his only son, and if he assists her, she will support his sone in becoming the mayor of one of the cities!

Sadly, Natural's own blood was betraying her! Her aunt was seeking retribution for some past wrongdoing.

Shaadi wanted Natural to suffer the sorrows that her own brother had inflicted on her.

I suppose this was the only way to calm her down in her thoughts!

Even though I knew the facts, I was powerless to aid Natural. Shaadi was pointing the finger at both of us!

While I was sitting in the garden one day, I received a letter that had been tossed to my house. It was a detective's message.

He requested that we meet at one of the cafés. I had to switch automobiles four times until they were certain the cops had completely lost track of me!

It was difficult to get away from them; I was lucky that they couldn't track me after the third car because I swapped clothes with a guy who was the same size as me, he went with the taxi, and I stayed until I was sure they were following him, then I came out, got a cap, and went to the final stop!

When I arrived at the restaurant, it was located near the psychological hospital. When I first walked in, I realized that Prince Albert was dressed in a disguise, so no one could tell who he was.

The detective was also present, and he was accompanied by a large contingent of security. Only three of us were inside, and we were guarded from the outside!

He motioned for me to have a seat, then stated that we share one trait, which is Natural!

That was the reason, he added, that I had been summoned. He was ready to allow Natural out of the hospital, but he had a condition: I had to let her go!

I was afraid of losing her, but how could I refuse him when he was Natural's final hope? For her, I was willing to sacrifice my life.

The detective then sat down and discussed their plan. He stated that she would be discharged the following day, and Albert would accompany her.

According to him, the hospital will face charges for illegally holding Natural, and the doctor has already been detained.

Shaadi had been away for a few days, and her spy may have alerted her about Albert's pursuit, leading her to prepare her escape.

I asked him to just let me see her from a distance, and he consented for the last time.

They were going to collect her in the morning, even though it was nearly midnight.

Albert informed me that I could sleep in a camper van.

Then he asked, "What would you do if you were in my situation?"

I responded by telling him that "To be honest, I'm not sure, but I don't believe you could have done anything other! Thank you for assisting her."

"Actually, it's difficult to say, even if you had agreed to what Albert wanted, there was no guarantee that she would be safe. After all, Albert had been looking forward to this opportunity to be with her! or maybe he was acting the whole time while working with Shaadi!" I informed Sir Malik.

"Albert had requested that international police seek for her, and there are also rewards for anyone who can discover or report her!"

Then he went on to say, "So the day of my dread arrived, and the operation began." Outside the hospital, there were a few police cars.

It was the detective who was in charge! Albert tried to hide his face and remained inside, but they let me stand in the corner and wait for Natural from a distance.

She was wheeled out of the hospital, but, according to the detective, she had no recollection of anything or anyone at the time. She thought they were supposed to take her to the city hospital for a check-up.

I couldn't believe my eyes when I saw her that day. The lovely angel, her hair shorn and dressed in a hospital gown, was looking about and longing for a familiar face!

I wanted to scream and tell her I was right there with her, just ten steps away, but I couldn't.

I'm not sure I'd ever sobbed as much as I did that day!

Then she vanished totally, till...

He then indicated that he couldn't go any farther since I should know what she remembers and inform me.

He predicted that it would be difficult for her, but that it would be beneficial in the end.

Her doctor claims that if she can remember, her pain will subside, and she will be the one to remember it.

I agreed with him and asked them if I might leave early because my father was not feeling well.

Sir Malik offered me a ride, and Natural gave me all of the home cooked meals that she had prepared for us! What a beautiful couple they are!

My father was considerably better, and I believe that after seeing all those foods, he regained his appetite.

Since he nearly completed everything, took a shower, and went to bed early!

I went to our room's balcony and began contemplating what Sir Malik had said to me today!

What a horrific scene, Natural, and what a huge price she had to pay for her vengeance!

She was held responsible for something that had nothing to do with her flaws.

Shaadi was the one who should have been admitted to a psychology facility instead of her. Who could possibly do something so heinous to her own blood?

That night, I was reflecting on how some people's life become complicated all of a sudden.

How far should they go to achieve peace?

What was Natural's pay for happiness? I was irritated and furious because what Shaadi had done to her niece was not right!

# Chapter 16
# The Alternate Route

My father got over his cold the next day. He was curious as to when we would be able to return home because he missed my mother.

I told him we were almost done with the story, but we'd gotten to the point when Natural needed some assistance remembering things, and Sir Malik was doing his best.

I told him that this isn't just a story; it's also Natural's road to rehabilitation.

My father was intrigued about what I was talking about, but I told him he would have to wait!

He accompanied me to the door and thanked Natural for the delicious supper she had prepared.

He then told her that since he was going to an old friend's house, I was hers for the day.

If I want, he said I can stay. He'll pick me up once he finishes.

My father appeared skeptical, but that was fine; I didn't want to be obnoxious by asking him all the time.

Natural was ill, and she refused to continue the story, but Sir Malik insisted on seeing it through.

He intended to write the story a few years ago, she claimed, but she was the one who always blocked him.

Then he said this year, "Let's get another author to write our story so we can both talk about the past and say whatever we want."

"You folks chose me to create the narrative!" "Truly, I was so lucky!" That's what I said.

She stated that, while she is still unwilling to continue the story, she does not wish to keep me waiting any longer!

Then she invited me to come to the room where she used to stay as a housekeeper.

Before I could express any questions, she confirmed that everything was still the same!

She expressed her desire for them to begin modifying everything in each area after she concludes the story.

I took a seat in the chair, while she took a seat on the bed.

"I'm not ready to get started since I'm not sure what to say. I'll make every effort not to overlook anything," said Natural.

I honestly can't remember the day Albert and his guys came and grabbed me.

They took me in a big van and dropped me off in a different section of town after a few hours.

My doctors switched, and I started using a new drug that made me feel more awake.

I was constantly being examined.

Albert was worried that if Shaadi had requested them, they would have done major damage to my skull during the surgery, but they had merely opened it and then put it back together.

Shaadi probably just wanted to prove to me that she could do worse, but she won't!

Albert was with me the majority of the time. When he wasn't around, he'd ask his guards to keep me safe in his castle, and I wasn't permitted to leave.

I begged him a few times to hunt for Malik on my behalf, and the only response I got was that he had changed his location.

He was also suspected of kidnapping Shaadi's daughter, according to authorities.

Then he recounted me the entire tale, with minor alterations that he made to make it even worse!

One day, I informed him, "Shaadi has gone, and her allegation against Malik is definitely no longer genuine," so why doesn't he go locate Malik and inform him so he can resume his normal life?

He became enraged and stated emphatically that he was the one who was looking after me and keeping me safe.

He was the one who saved me from the mental institution and returned me to my normal life. Why am I not seeing what he's done and still searching for Malik?

I told him that I adore him and that every day I hope to hear his voice once more.

That aspect was really difficult for him to comprehend, and it enraged him greatly.

I spent six months at his detention center. I couldn't do it anymore because he wanted me to start flying on his private aircraft and take him wherever I wanted.

He couldn't understand why I was sad. I needed Malik and his warm shoulder, not the gorgeous castle or the services he was delivering.

I told him I couldn't give him my heart.

I knew he was the one who had spared me from everything, but I couldn't pretend to love him as he deserved.

I could see his sad expression and all of his tears. He refused to quit up since he was so arrogant. I adored him, but I couldn't take Malik's place.

He claimed he would return my freedom to me on my birthday night, and he did.

He claimed that his father had died and that he was now a king.

I told him he was the best, true friend I had ever had, and he was heartbroken that he couldn't win my heart. I'll always adore him, and our tie is unshakable.

That night, he kissed me, and I somehow let him! He had earned it.

I had a dream that Sir's entire house was on fire one night.

I awoke in a pool of perspiration, then began to recall the girl from my nightmares; she was the one from the newspaper.

Shaadi's daughter was the one the cops were hunting for!

Albert was asked if he could assist me with some information about Shaadi's daughter.

Did Shaadi ever inform you her daughter was deaf, he asked one day? or was Elizabeth's name changed to Pleasure after she was given away?

**Oh, my goodness.**

So it was her all along, she was the one on the lookout for me! She was requesting assistance since she had gone missing!

She asked me to track her down! But how do you do it?

Then I began recounting Albert the story from the beginning, explaining how he had changed dramatically since becoming a king.

He was quite helpful and once asked why I hadn't told Malik or even him about it.

No one could have believed me when I stated I was afraid of being judged. But, after hearing about Shaadi and her missing daughter, and rather than blaming Malik or even myself, I believe this is something serious, and we should investigate further!

It was Christmas, and Albert was about to be proclaimed king and introduced to the entire public in the new year.

He requested Malik to come and join us, and he gave me the best gift of my life!

When I spotted him in the main hall, I nearly had a heart attack with joy.

He looked as attractive as ever, but my heart rate was probably above 200, so I couldn't say anything.

I just ran up to him and he hugged me, and we both started crying. Albert was looking at us, and we were both silently enjoying the warm embrace.

He was there that day, keeping an eye on you from afar!

Albert concluded by saying, "We both really proved it to him," implying that true love still exists, despite what we see in movies or read in books.

He stated that he tried everything he could to capture my heart, but he was unsuccessful!

Then he stepped closer to both of us and said, "I came to realize I am his only trustworthy friend in the entire world, and all this time he was erroneously asking for the wrong thing," he added. "He stated he had my companionship, which Malik couldn't have, and it is for a lifetime!"

He stated that he will assist Malik in the search for the missing girl, allowing us to finally spend time together.

I was ecstatic that day, but I was terrified of celebrating. At any minute, I was expecting Shaadi would emerge from one of the rooms and take me away from him, or Albert would become evil again and try to punish us!

Malik proposed to me that night, saying he didn't want to waste any more time; I had been waiting for this moment since the first time I saw him!

He asked if I was okay with him being of a different religion. I didn't mind at all because we all believed in the same God who reunited us.

We married on Christmas Day, having Albert as our witness; the next day, we left the palace, and Albert returned.

When I walked into the house, practically all of my memories came flooding back, both good and horrible, especially nightmares!

Malik was completely unaware of what was going on in his home.

After we'd settled in, I told him about the girl and reminded him of everything that had been going on.

He told me that he didn't feel alone in the house, and that he could hear something but couldn't pinpoint what it was.

He claimed he had already told Jamal about his visions, but that he was feeling this way because of stress!

That night, Malak and I talked a lot about the past; I'd been telling him about it since the day I first saw PLEASURE!

He also admitted that he was taken aback when he discovered some baby garments in my room, a shattered window, and a message with only one word 'Help' written on it.

He said something to the effect that if his house was haunted, why was she visiting me in Shaadi's castle or even the hospital?

As a result, it had little to do with his home I felt. He told me that I was talented, and that while he was training on his own, part of their work included the ability to perceive other souls, which was perfectly normal.

He stated, "I was picked, and that is why she came to see me!"

# Chapter 17
# Final Is Not the End

Natural remarked, turning to face me, "We used to be terrified of ghosts, but now it was more like a science or puzzle."

I felt angry with myself for keeping such a significant matter a secret for so long.

Malik was really understanding; I was the one passing judgment because he seemed to be taking the whole thing in stride.

If I were in her shoes, I couldn't initiate a conversation with someone about these topics, I informed her.

since I wasn't sure how they would have responded!

Their psyche was prepared to absorb additional pleasure after all that had occurred!

You must have believed that everything you were seeing or hearing was just a vision or voice in your brain since you couldn't tell whether it was a nightmare or reality and you had been treated like a patient at your aunt's place.

I still believe that holding it to yourself until the appropriate moment was the proper move. I told Natural that.

My perception of her improved as I noticed that she was grinning. My viewpoint was shared by her.

Then exhaled deeply and remarked, "I suppose you have a point, and I truly loved it."

The police were no longer keeping an eye on Malik, but his case was still opened, she said.

The detective came to see us one day on Albert's instruction, and he requested us to start at the beginning and go into detail about everything.

He was comfortably situated and listening to both sides of the story.

When a class was coming up for Pleasure, he asked Malik if he had a housekeeper or anyone else who could go to the residence with ease.

Malik confirmed that he had assistance, and she departed the job claiming that there was too much to do and she was only getting a meager wage.

He then departed after asking for some time to conduct additional research.

I was sleeping in Malik's room, he was in the front room—his office!

Our beds remained separate even after we got married, and I was terrified and struggling with my body image, particularly how I looked.

He wasn't really complaining, and we were both content.

My hair had reached my shoulders and covered the scar. I had lost a lot of weight, since I was still sick and had to throw up everything I had eaten the previous day.

According to the doctors, my rehabilitation will take longer than anticipated!

Every time a plane flew overhead, I lost control and started crying.

Sadly, they declined to take me back. I tried so hard, but they had every right to reject me because, first of all, I was a woman and, second, they weren't really interested in hiring a Pilot with a brain injury and personality problems.

I used to take advantage of Albert's private jets once or twice a week, occasionally by myself and usually with Malik.

We would travel for two or three hours before returning.

I constantly say "thank you" to him for letting me do all of that. Even though it is against the law, I still do it since it actually helped me get healthier.

Malik was giving up on taking lessons outside the home and was only working from home since he wanted to be present at all times.

He helped me stand up by doing a number of things.

When I returned from Albert Castle, I had no idea where I was at all. Without Malik, I'm not sure what I would have done.

My path back to normalcy and becoming me again was illuminated by his love.

Everything he wrote—poems, books, paintings—was about me! He eventually realized that he was only writing about me.

I got the impression that everything there was mostly about me because of the atmosphere he generated.

I was once more significant, attractive, intelligent, and most importantly, loved.

Malik came and slept next to my bed on the ground one night when I had a high fever and went to bed early.

I heard someone calling my name in the middle of the night.

She was there at the door when I awoke. I checked to see whether Malik was still asleep before getting out of bed, going outside, and calling her by her real name and telling her I knew who she was.

I informed her that I was her cousin, that I was aware of her backstory, and that I knew her mother.

Shaadi has been punishing Malik as a result of her.

She was silent, not reacting or talking. She then asked me to accompany her to the garden.

She was indicating with her fingers a particular location where I had recently planted some flowers.

Then she abruptly disappeared. I got there and began digging because someone was pulling me to there; it was out of my control.

Even though it was still dark and I couldn't see anything, I didn't care. All I wanted to know was why she was pointing there and if there was anything there—a suitcase, a letter, or something else—that may help us locate her.

The clang of a bell interrupted us as Natural moved to open the gate and I was scanning the space.

I noticed that Sir Malik had two large food containers and a few bags with him.

We have a guest tonight, he added as I stepped outside to assist him.

Natural was to sit with me while I finished the story; he didn't want her to go into the kitchen and start cooking.

Natural also appeared astonished, and I was certain that she was unaware that they had a visitor!

Anyway, I gave them some space before returning to the room.

I was extremely hungry and it was already the afternoon.

Before Neutral returned, it didn't take long. I quickly finished the sandwich she handed me and was prepared for her to begin the story as she had two sandwiches with her.

She prompted me to eat more, but I declined, thanking her instead and stating that there would be plenty of time to eat later because she would soon be busy.

Then she started:

Malik came across me in the garden digging with my hands, he had no idea what to do, he asked me what had occurred, I told him Pleasure wanted me to inspect this location, and he immediately began assisting me.

He instructed me to stop and asked for his shovel, and he will handle the rest!

When he realized he could no longer dig, he stopped and turned to face me.

There was sufficient light to see everything because daylight was almost here.

He want me to go inside, but I persisted and discovered a human skull there!

I just sat on the ground and nearly yelled; my tears were non-stop. Malik led me inside the residence and made an effort to get me something to drink; he said he was unaware that a body was buried inside.

After some time, I instructed him to notify the detective by phone.

He followed suit, and within 30 minutes the entire team arrived at our residence along with an ambulance to remove the body!

Nobody spoke to us at all! The detective arrived later in the evening than expected.

Malik was sent to the police station for more inquiry! Along with him, I went.

In the evening, a detective arrived and escorted us to his office. He apologized for being late and explained that the reason he should have waited so long was because he was working on our case and was awaiting DNA results.

Our house was locked by the police, so he requested us to go to the hotel tonight.

He claimed he was unable to speak at this time since the results had not yet been released, but that by tomorrow all will be obvious.

We checked into the motel that evening, but neither of us could sleep until dawn.

There was a dead body in Malik's garden, and he was constantly inconsolable about it.

After breakfast, a police car pulled up outside of our hotel and drove us back to the police station.

Detective urged us to sit down when he saw us waiting in the room.

He observed our anxious expressions and assured us that, if we could only settle down, he would be able to speak with us.

We sat down, and he said: He claimed that following our last encounter, he went in search of Sir's former home kipper; he eventually located her, and after much threatening, she finally began to speak!

She was almost always present when Sir had a private lesson. The maid has picked up on Samuel and Pleasure's covert relationship.

He claimed that although the two appeared 30 minutes early for the session and pretended to be practicing their art in the antique room, Samuel was actually assaulting Pleasure.

Natasha had no idea about that because Samuel was attempting to play it cool and maintain both relationships with both girls.

She claimed that when she initially heard Pleasure screaming, she opened the antique door to see Samuel attempting to push her. She said she requested him to go, and he later gave her a large sum of money in exchange for keeping quiet.

The maid claimed that occasionally she would inquire about Sir's calendar before alerting Samuel so that he might enjoy visit the empty house!

Prior to Pleasure going missing one day, she claimed she overheard Mr. Samuel yelling at Pleasure, slapping her, and telling her to get an abortion.

When she realized that, she decided it was time to quit her job.

She couldn't handle it any longer, so she requested Samuel to give her a large sum of money so she could quit!

She claimed that she had tried to work with Samuel because, as a single mother of four children, she genuinely needed the money.

After receiving a check from Samuel, she will claim that her pay is inadequate and that she will no longer be coming.

She did, however, note that she returned to Sir's residence the night of the accident to collect up her final salary from Sir Malik.

She discovered there was a fire, had a key, and saw a girl fleeing toward the pool. She was so terrified that she didn't even bother to go inside; instead, she fled right away and has never come back.

Sir was dreadfully distressed. Sad to learn that his home has been the scene of such terrible things!

"When Pleasure refused to get an abortion, Samuel allegedly threatened to kill her. It's possible that he did so in an effort to frighten her, but sadly, the threat came true, and Pleasure was fatally burned," Detective pointed.

She may have been spotted rushing by the maid when she was running from the hall to the backyard garden to jump into the pool.

*She will jump into the pool, and by the time Samuel gets there and tries to save her, it will be too late (there was a black flame on the hallway ceiling),* assumed the detective.

"She will be lifted and kept on the sofa that was left outside the garden by him. I believe Sir kept it out because it needed repair or was broken."

On the sofa, we discovered the burnt remnant of her body.

Samuel dug a hole in the garden and buried Pleasure's body there because he was helpless to do anything else at the time.

Then he would drain the pool completely, wash the couch, and tidy up the house.

Samuel will visit Natasha that evening after speaking with her mother. Given that she had a cold, he will act concerned for her health and ask if they will let her go outside for a short while.

They'll take a brief drive after.

No one knows what transpired in the automobile between them, but we assume he told Natasha all that had occurred.

They got into an argument with her, lost control of the vehicle, and were involved in a fatal accident.

These are all just assumptions, but they may all be astonishingly accurate or not.

I questioned him over Shaadi, to which he replied, "She was chasing Sir Malik for a long time, but she didn't know how to get to his residence."

She had requested Jamal to offer you the job, so in this way, by tracking you, she could easily keep an eye on Sir Malik and his actions. "You (Natural)made the way easy for her, after she found out, about your interest in Sir's book and trying to find him."

"You falling in love with Sir surprised Shaadi, and that just strengthened her resolve to seek punishment." he mentioned.

On that day, we kept replaying in our minds everything that had occurred during the previous few months.

Both Sir and I were shocked by Pleasure and her relationship with Samuel. Sir was really disappointed.

I started going back in time and attempting to relate everything she had shown me to reality.

She wanted to tell me she was pregnant because so many of them matched, especially the newborn clothing!

That night, the fire! Honestly, I saw her, she was burning, I helped her, and she was sitting on the couch.

I was present in the antique room and I witnessed everything!

Natural then began to cry uncontrollably because of the pain she was feeling inside.

The only thing I could find to make her feel better was to start crying myself.

Unfortunately, whether I liked it or not, the ending was true, contrary to what I had anticipated.

I informed Natural that now was the time to let go.

Both of them were in great pain.

Then I got up and assisted Natural in getting ready for her guests by going to get some rest.

When I returned, Sir was busy cleaning the berries and setting the table in the garden.

He asked me if Natural could complete it after glancing at me.

I confirmed that she had finished it.

After being freed, he declared that he could now sell the house. Natural, who had previously been provisioned, appeared to be refusing to let him sell the residence.

It was difficult to overcome all of those pains, Sir said, but one of us needed to be stronger and move forward, and that was me. I could tell he was happy by the look on his face.

After asking me to sit, he gave me coffee, sat next to me, and said: "However, Natural returned to her phases after that day." She stopped eating once again and blamed herself for not assisting her because she wasn't getting any visits from Pleasure anymore, which hurt her.

She claimed that she had treated Pleasure improperly the previous time she had seen her.

She felt let down by her family. Although I was always nearby, she was crying because her aunt had let her fall.

She needed six months to recover her strength and start over in life.

God alone knows how I survived these months. Her warm hands, wonderful heart, and compassionate disposition were the only things that gave me hope.

Even though Jamal was wealthy from the Shaadi and had gotten his portion, he had no desire to return to his country.

I am afraid that one day Shaadi may return to get us because she is still gone and no one has seen her.

Her late husband's family took all of her possessions! Natural has only received a little portion of what she pledged to the orphanage where Pleasure was reared. After learning the truth about Pleasure, Shaadi might have felt heartbroken.

"I had a hard time accepting that my house had been damaged so badly by individuals I trusted. It made me think of my father and the shady relationships he had with his pupils." stated Sir.

Natural continues to visit her doctor once a week; all those medications, sadly, had adverse effects.

She had been physically and emotionally involved in the surgery, which had also hurt a few nerves, so I couldn't expect her to recover quickly. I was willing to handle worse because I love her!

When the time came, I figured having a child or adopting one would assist her, but she refused, saying she was afraid that if we got into an accident, Shaadi would be to blame and the child would be left all by himself without a parent! She is unable to move on from her darkest nightmare regarding her aunt.

If I could only persuade her to let us to write our narrative, perhaps by sharing it with the world, the sorrow from the past would be reduced.

"She couldn't talk to me the way she wanted, especially when she wanted to speak about Albert or Pleasure's visits," he continued.

"Since this is ultimately about her and not about me, I wanted her to be herself and speak freely. She had given everything up."

"She had given everything up."

I was requested to check on Natural by Sir Malik. She was not in when I walked upstairs and knocked on her door.

I knocked again, and this time Natural asked me to enter. I could hear two people talking, one of whom was Natural, but the other I couldn't identify was undoubtedly a lady.

Natural claimed to be talking to Pleasure when I arrived to check on her after finding her to be alone.

She claimed that she had visited Pleasure for the first time in a very long time and that Pleasure had brought Natasha along with her since she seemed so pleased.

They both appreciated my efforts in spreading the word about this incident, as did you.

I could actually hear the voices of two individuals, albeit it was a little unsettling. I simply grinned at her and said, "Welcome, sweetie."

"Sir inquired as to your well-being."

I couldn't speak and had no idea what to do, so the most I could manage at the time was to try not to act ridiculous.

After that, Natural felt more at ease, so she came down with me and told Sir the same thing about Pleasure and Natasha's visits! Sir Malik asked whether he might sell the house now that she was satisfied. She replied, "Yes."

Sir Malik expressed his delight and promised to get assistance from a buddy who works in real estate.

Natural were wearing a green gown, and as previously, her red hair was long and smooth.

Being with her always made me feel relaxed since she had something extremely special about her. She was pleased to find that Sir Malik had completed the task.

She asked Sir to be with me and said she would handle everything from there.

The gallery that Sir Malik had previously shown me to was where he wanted me to go.

I was waiting to go back when he told me to guess who was there after removing the covers from a few photographs that he had already completed.

They were named Samuel, Natasha, and Pleasure under their photographs, so I recognized them as being a young man and two women. Everyone was present. I sensed that everyone was gazing at me!

Natural was the one who did all that, and after that, she never painted or drew anything again, Sir remarked, so he asked me not to panic.

It took me some time to process what he said.

It seemed a little weird, but since I was aware of their background, I could comprehend it better.

Sir gave me a wonderful surprise, and it was my own portrait, which he had painted and signed. I gave him a hug but didn't know how to express my gratitude for the chance he had given me.

He also complimented me for making the effort to stay in the hotel with my Dad all these days, saying he couldn't wait for me to put all I heard in words.

My dad had already arrived. wanted to go and reserve our tickets for the following day, despite Natural's insistence that we both stay for the party.

She gave me a hug and said I was the actual support and inspiration she needed. I didn't want to leave them, but my heart was heavy. We quickly grew quite close, and they began to believe that I was a part of their family.

I informed Sir that I would phone them if I had any questions, and I extended an invitation for them to come stay with us over the next holiday.

Natural and Sir Malik were bid farewell by both of us.

Like those who had worked out for five hours, I was exhausted. My body was worn out.

As soon as we arrived back at our house, I went straight to my room and almost slept for two days.

My mother was shocked; she had assumed I was ill. I suppose my brain was in need of a rest at the moment.

# Chapter 18
# From the Author to the Readers

This book was a fresh portal into a different realm, regardless of whether you want to call it reality or just what has always been classified as fiction!

After getting to know Sir Malik and his lady, I gained a better understanding of my situation and our surroundings.

I never thought that a soul could have a relationship with anyone in this world since I've been told that everything is a deception.

After what I seen and witnessed, I began to consider more carefully and changed my mind. Natural was an emotional control freak who would gracefully accept her gift. Her husband was one of the few people who truly understood her, and this created a strong bond between them.

How beautifully two distinct persons practicing two different religions arrived next to one another!

Natural had no control over the events that occurred to her.

She was punished as well as accused of committing a crime that she didn't believe.

There must be a huge number of people out there that experience the same criticism, hatred, and rejection every single day, even from their own people and bloodline.

Natural had no intention of returning to get revenge on those who had combined to treat her so horribly after what she had gone through, not even once.

She was merely relieved to be standing again and to have her partner at her side. She served as an inspiration for me and all other ladies to never give up.

For me, Sir Malik continues to be an example of a real man. He was a good lover, strong, knowledgeable, and emotional all at once!

Although I don't think Natural's circumstances were simple to comprehend, he didn't perceive any of those things but his love.

It got to the point where he stopped caring about things like beauty, money, status, and prestige. Nothing else was on his wish list other than to be with her.

But the whole goal of bringing this book to life is to make you think twice once you've finished reading it.

I've been told that seeing is believing. Don't forget that just because we can't see something doesn't imply it doesn't exist.

I went through the procedure once more and finished the second book.

I genuinely hope you all find it useful.

Thank you all so much.
We'll cross paths again.
Love.
Yalda